all
the
beloved
ghosts

all
the
beloved
ghosts
Alison
MacLeod

B L O O M S B U R Y

LONDON · OXFORD · NEW YORK · NEW DELHI · SYDNEY

Bloomsbury Publishing
An imprint of Bloomsbury Publishing Plc

50 Bedford Square
London
WC1B 3DP
UK

1385 Broadway
New York
NY 10018
USA

www.bloomsbury.com

BLOOMSBURY and the Diana logo are trademarks of Bloomsbury Publishing Plc

First published in Great Britain 2017

British Library Cataloguing-in-Publication Data
A catalogue record for this book is available from the British Library.

ISBN:	HB:	978-1-4088-6375-6
	TPB:	978-1-4088-6376-3
	EPUB:	978-1-4088-6377-0

2 4 6 8 10 9 7 5 3 1

Typeset by Integra Software Services Pvt. Ltd.
Printed and bound in Great Britain by CPI Group (UK) Ltd, Croydon CR0 4YY

To find out more about our authors and books visit www.bloomsbury.com.
Here you will find extracts, author interviews, details of forthcoming
events and the option to sign up for our newsletters.

For Ian, Anne, Kath and Ellen, with love

Contents

The Thaw

For Marjorie Genevieve

Wisdom after the event is cheap indeed – but go back.

The smoky light of a March sunrise is seeping through the winter drapes. Outside, the world is glassy; the trees on Pleasant Street, glazed with winter. Every bare branch, every dead leaf is sheathed in ice, like a fossil from another age, an antediluvian dream of blossom and green canopies. Below her bedroom window, the drifts rise up in frozen waves of white – even the sudden gusts and eddies of wind cannot disturb those peaks – while overhead, the warmth of the sun is so reluctant in its offerings, so meagre, you'd not be alone if you failed to notice the coming of the first thaw.

Above her room, a sheet of ice on the eaves gives way, smashing like a mirror on to the porch roof, but everyone in the house sleeps on. Marjorie – or Marjorie Genevieve as her father always called her – sleeps in what the family still call 'Ethel's room', though it has been thirteen years since Ethel was taken from them by TB. Ethel, 1913. And Kathleen, just two years later, only twenty-two. Marjorie still keeps one of Kathleen's Sunday handkerchiefs, spotted with her blood.

As for their mother, Cecelia Maud, it is true what people say. She has never recovered from the deaths of her three grown children: Ethel, Kathleen and, finally, senselessly, Murray, two months after Kathleen. Before Christmas, Marjorie found her mother sitting in the ice house with her coat unbuttoned and sawdust stuck to the bare soles of her feet.

After seven daughters, Providence gave Cecelia Maud and James MacLeod a single son, a boy who would become the youngest lawyer ever admitted to the Bar in the province of Nova Scotia.

Some say the MacLeods hold themselves too high – which is perhaps why the fight broke out, behind Batterson's Dry Goods, which, everyone knew, doubled as a bootlegger's after dark on Saturdays.

No man that night would ever say who was involved or who threw the first punch. Only this was clear. Murray was laid out on a table in the storeroom. Concussed, they said, that was all. Come morning, he'd have a devil of a sore head, and a hard time defending himself to his mother and his wife, lawyer or no. Louis Clarke, the town's Inspector, gave them ten minutes while he turned a blind eye, stepped outside and marvelled, as he was known to do, at the plenitude of stars in the Cape Breton sky. Two men, suddenly stark sober, heaved Murray into their arms. They took the short cut through Plant's Field; saw only the Portuguese fishermen who were camped, as ever, by the brook, their damp clothes hanging pale as spectres, while their owners slept.

That Sunday morning in August, Cecelia Maud woke early. She planned to pick a few Little Gem lettuces from the garden before they wilted in the day's heat. But when she opened the inside door of the back porch, she found her only son slumped against the rocker, blood seeping from his ear.

It was only after the clockwork of the day had begun – the stove swept (no char on a Sunday), the breakfast table laid – that Marjorie found her mother on the floor beside her brother, and for a moment she struggled to know the living from the dead.

But no charges were laid. No notice of the funeral was given in St Joseph's weekly bulletin. It was an unusually quiet gathering, family only, for Murray MacLeod was the youngest lawyer ever to be called to the Bar – dead after a Saturday night at the bootlegger's.

The town whispered. Such a shame. Hadn't the family already been locked away in their years of mourning? Those girls would hardly know themselves when the black sheets came off the mirrors.

But the MacLeods, Catholic, suffered their most recent loss privately. With three daughters of the house yet to be married, the family remained aware: they were fortunate to reside on Pleasant Street, in the enviable, Protestant district of Ward One.

Again. *Wisdom after the event is cheap indeed* – but these words and the article itself, in the *North Sydney Herald*, are still unimaginable. As she wakes this Saturday morning in a frozen March, Marjorie Genevieve is enjoying the knowledge that her coat was anything but cheap.

She works Mondays and Wednesdays at the head office of Thompson's Foundry. Before her father died, he made it clear he would consent to a part-time position only. She did not *need* to work, he explained with a benign smile, and although James MacLeod is now eight years gone, no one, not even Marjorie's eldest sister, May, with her fierce intelligence and heavy eyebrows, has the authority to overturn his decision.

Marjorie knew it had to be beaver, not muskrat, not even muskrat dyed to look like mink.

A three-quarter-length, wrap-round coat in unsheared beaver.

She saved for two years.

In the darkness of her room, she neither turns on the lamp nor removes the mourning sheet from her cheval mirror. She slides the coat on over her night-gown and rubs her palm against the nape of the fur. The sensation of it is enough. The shawl collar tickles her bare neck. The silk lining is cool against her chest. When she pulls back the drapes, she can see almost nothing of the day through the bedroom window. The pane is a palimpsest of frost; the world is white. But she is radiantly warm.

It is only right. There has been enough grief. Thirteen years of grief. Ethel. Kathleen. Murray. Then her father. Is it any wonder that her mother is the husk of herself? But she, Marjorie, is *twenty-nine*.

Wearing the fur over only her nightgown, Marjorie feels nearly naked.

The furrier at Vooght Brothers had the voice of an orator. 'I do not need to persuade you of the elegance of this coat. But remember, while beaver is sometimes known for being heavy to wear, it offers *exceptional* protection against the excesses of a Cape Breton winter. Notice how the long guard hairs give this coat its lustrous sheen.'

She noticed.

He took the liberty of easing the coat over her shoul-ders. The drape felt exquisite; the weight of the fur, a strange new gravity. A lining of gold dress-silk flashed within. She wrapped the coat around herself, and felt the dense animal softness mould itself to her form.

'You won't find a more fashionable cut this side of Montreal.'

It was the coat of a mature, stylish woman, the coat of a woman of nearly thirty.

She deposited her payment in a small metal box and watched it whiz away on an electric wire. Within moments, the box came sailing back down the line, and revealed, as if by magic, her bill of sale.

Her account was settled.

The coat would be delivered.

The dance was Saturday night.

The penalties of past mistakes cannot be remitted, but at least the lessons so solemnly and dearly learned should be taken to heart.

But not yet. Wait—

Because Charlie Thompson is pulling up next to the hitching rail outside Vooght's, where William Dooley, the funeral director, has stopped his team. Steam rises from the horses' flanks as a small group of men – from Dooley's, the Cable Office, the Vendome Hotel and the Royal Albert – gather to offer, with low whistles and eagle eyes, their unreserved admiration for Charlie Thompson's new 1926 Buick Roadster.

Marjorie sees him – Mr Thompson, her employer – and nods briefly before turning right when, in fact, she meant to turn left for home. But it's too late. Her pride in her new purchase has distracted her, and she doesn't want to walk past the group of men again straightaway, so she slips into the Royal Café and orders tea with a slice of Lady Baltimore cake.

Outside the gleaming window, a single, tusky icicle drips, one of a long row that hangs from the café's awning, though Marjorie does not notice this first sign of the coming spring.

Between sips of tea, she watches the gathering across the street. William Dooley, the funeral director, has eased himself into the driver's seat. Mr Thompson is leaning on the door of the Buick, showing him the inner sanctum, but even so, he is taller than the others. She supposes he's handsome for a man of his age: dark-haired, grey only at the temples, an easy smile. Shame about the one short leg. A birth defect, she was told.

According to Eleanor in the office, he always walks fast, trying to disguise it, and his tailor 'gets hell' if the hem of his trousers doesn't hide the top of his block of a shoe. 'Maybe the bad leg's the reason he likes *speed*,' Eleanor murmured, leaning forward. 'Well, there's that new automobile, isn't there? Plus some fine breed of horse up at the racecourse.' She lowered her chin and whispered into her bosom. 'Apparently, he's a *gambler*.'

Maybe, thought Marjorie. But married, fifty, sober, Protestant, well off, with three children. Respectable.

She leaves two bites of cake on her plate, as May taught her. Then she pushes in her chair, slips on her wool coat and pays the bill. Across the street, Charlie Thompson has resumed the ordinary shape of the man who lopes unevenly past her desk each morning while the secretaries, Marjorie included, lower their eyes out of courtesy.

As she slips through the door of the Royal Café, there can be no way for Marjorie to know that the man she is about to pass for the second time that day – Charlie

Thompson, married, fifty, Protestant, with three children – is her future.

On Route 28, the chains on the car's tires grip the snowy twists and bends. They hum, then clunk, with every rotation, a primitive rhythm that sends Marjorie into a world of her own. It's a sixteen-mile journey from North Sydney to Sydney, and, wrapped in her new coat, she enjoys every moment, staring through her window at the frozen expanse of Sydney Harbour, mesmerised by its white, elemental glow.

So she makes only the poorest of efforts to shout over the engine for chit-chat with Eleanor and Eleanor's brother, Stan, up front. The forty-minute journey passes in what seems like ten, and in no time, the flaming tower of Sydney's steelworks looms into view, spitting like a firework.

The *Herald* will assure us that, as she arrives at the Imperial Hotel on Sydney's Esplanade, Marjorie is *a young lady* whose thoughts are *centred on an evening's innocent recreation*. In the lobby, she passes her fur to the cloak-room attendant, wondering if the girl will be tempted to try it on when no one's looking. *Go on*, she wants to say. *I don't mind!* But she doesn't want to presume.

'Don't forget your dance cards!' the girl calls after them, and Marjorie dashes back.

For this is a dance, not a society ball, and Marjorie thrills to the faint promise of the unexpected, the spontaneous. Stan is their chaperone, and if he is necessary, he is also negligible.

On the threshold of the hotel's ballroom, she tries to compose a picture in her mind to savour tomorrow morning. But it's a kaleidoscope. The colour of the dresses. (All the satin!) The candlelight from the tables. The glassy polish of the men's shoes. The gleam of the instruments on stage.

Then Eleanor is nudging her arm and reciting the names of the dances marked on their cards. How they laugh. There's the Turkey Trot, the Wiggle-de-Wiggle, the Shorty George, the Fuzzy Wuzzy . . . Sixteen dances in all. They sashay into the ballroom. 'I hope I've got a little Negro in my blood,' shouts Eleanor, and Marjorie forces a smile, not knowing the polite reply. Besides, the twelve-man band has started to bugle and strum, to sway and trombone, and Marjorie knows this one – 'Everything's Gonna Be Alright' .

'There must be more than five hundred people here,' Eleanor marvels.

At a small round table, in a row of tables along a curving sweep of wall, Marjorie swaps her winter boots for her Mary Janes. 'And at least half are from North Sydney!' She didn't expect to feel so glad of the sight of all the familiar faces. The fluttering in her stomach eases.

'I told you we wouldn't be stuck with Stan all night. Besides, there are enough men from the KoC to mean that even the Pope himself would approve of our Turkey Trot. Look! Mr Thompson's here too.'

Marjorie spots him, smoking near the rear door. She nods and shrugs.

But Eleanor is squinting. 'He's here with the race-course set.'

'Is he?' and Marjorie turns to the band. Five of the twelve men are black. Two, the darkest black. She's heard there are Negro families in Sydney who have come all the way from the Deep South.

She's only ever seen a Negro once before, a stoker from the Foundry who came into the office because his wages were overdue. She liked the sound of his voice, the lazy music of his words.

Eleanor yells over the band. 'He's come on his own.'

'Who has?'

'*Mr Thompson*, silly. Mrs Thompson must be down with something. Not that it matters! He never dances anyway with that leg of his.'

Marjorie can see Stan crossing the floor towards them, refreshments in hand. In a moment, she tells herself, Eleanor will have another ear.

'Though you never know.' Eleanor giggles again and tugs at Marjorie's sleeve. 'The Shorty George might be just the number for him!'

Marjorie knows she should, but she doesn't care enough about Mr Thompson to protest on his behalf. Besides it's a new song now, one she's never heard – 'If You Can't Land 'Er on the Old Verandah' – and beneath her dress, her hips are already swaying.

Dance after dance, time is shimmying and quickstep-ping away, and Marjorie has no notion of the hour. She's red-faced and giddy from laughing through all the new steps, but the room still heaves with dancers. The men from the Boat Club are peeling off their jackets and climbing on top of each others' backs. Within moments, they're a teetering human pyramid, and, on the other side of the ballroom, Joe 'Clunk' McEwan is step-dancing on a tabletop to 'The Alabama Stomp'.

Behind her table, someone has propped open the rear doors for a blast of winter air, and hip flasks of bootlegged whisky are passing from man to man, across the dance floor. The MC is starting to slur, and the twelve-man band is three men down, but the music roars on. She has to pluck her dress away from her legs to catch any breath of air. The voice takes her completely by surprise. 'Excuse me, Miss. Is there room for one more on your dance card?'

Marjorie turns. One of the Negro men from the band – the double-bass player – is standing before her, his shoulders back, his tie loose at his neck. Where on earth did he spring from?

Beside her, Eleanor's head pivots on her neck; Marjorie sees her friend's hand fly to her chest. Stan takes a step forward.

She stands and blinks. She can see the man is not drunk. His eyes are clear; his gaze is steady if shy. For a moment, she wishes he were. Drunk. She might know what to do. She extends her hand. 'I'm enjoying the music, Mister . . . ?'

He nods, grinning at the parquet floor. 'I'm Walter. Would you like to dance, Miss?'

'Marjorie.' She clasps her palms. She can't think quickly enough. 'I have to confess, Walter. I'm done in for the night.'

'Tired?'

She nods. She wants to say, kindly, earnestly: *My good-ness, whatever has possessed you?* And she wants to say no such thing.

Walter still can't look up but he clicks his tongue. 'Tired? A fine dancer like you? I don't believe it. Why, you just need your second wind.'

A quiet sort of daring flashes from him. It warms her strangely. 'I'm sure it's none of my business, Walter, but are you one of the steelworkers from down south?' *Are the nights sultry?* she wants to ask. *Do the women carry fans?*

He nods. 'From Alabama, Miss.'

She wishes he would call her Marjorie. She will feel less rude when she sends him away. 'But Sydney's your home now?'

'Not Sydney proper, Miss.'

'No?'

'No.' He runs a hand across his chin and meets her eye. 'Me and my family, we live in Cokeville.'

She smiles politely. Then it comes to her: Cokeville. The area by Whitney Pier, where the filthy run-off from the coke ovens pours into the estuary.

The band strikes up a waltz, 'Wistful and Blue'. Walter offers her his hand, and she is surprised by the pale flash of his palms. The room is dark and packed, and who but Eleanor and Stan will really notice at this late hour? In any case, she *would* like to dance, she decides, and Walter's eyes spark with something she can't quite define.

As she accepts his hand, she feels the calluses on his fingertips. She has never met a double-bass player before. She does not see the heads at neighbouring tables turn in mid-sentence as she places her hand on his shoulder. Up close, Walter smells of lye, like the bar her mother keeps by the set tub.

From the seating area, there arises a low drone. She hears it dimly, beneath the melody. So she reaches after conversation, speaking into his ear. 'Did you bring your family with you to Sydney?'

He leads well. 'Yes, that's right. My mamma and my sisters.'

She dreads the eye of the roaming spotlight. 'That must be difficult – with just you to look after them, I mean.'

She can see his eyes assessing the risk: is it better to lead her into the shadows of the ballroom or to keep to the bright centre? 'Yes, Miss, I do my best. But it's been especially hard since my brother was killed.'

'Killed?' She stops dancing.

''Fraid so. Just before we left Alabama. At a speak-easy in our town. Leonard was hired to wash glasses. But a fight broke out over something or another that had gone missing. The manager was drunk. Went mad as a hornet. Broke a glass – on purpose like – and cut Leonard's throat.'

The shape of her brother Murray rises in Marjorie's mind's eye. Blood still seeps from his ear.

'Did they get the man, Walter, or did he get away?'

He swallows hard. 'Neither, Miss. They didn't get the man – and he didn't get away . . . That laid us low, my mamma especially.'

Marjorie nods. *Her mother. In the ice house. Her feet bare.*

Out of the corner of her eye, she notices that several of the men from the Knights of Columbus have risen from their chairs and now stand watching, their arms folded across their ties. They're wondering if Walter has offended her; if that's why she's having words. So she smiles at her partner, as if to say she is ready to dance again, and Walter waltzes her back into the music.

Couple after couple leave the dance floor. On stage, the MC stares through wide eyes and tries, with-out success, to catch the eye of the conductor. But

'Wistful and Blue' floats on into the wintery night – *one*, two, three – while the MC fiddles anxiously with his cuffs, and the ballroom of the Imperial Hotel empties. The KoC men, Marjorie notices, haven't returned to their tables, and Walter's hand has gone cold in hers.

The shadow of a tall man appears at the edge of the spotlight. Walter stops short. Marjorie squeezes her eyes shut. The air is about to break.

'May I?'

She opens her eyes to find Charlie Thompson standing before them. He has tapped Walter's shoulder.

Walter nods, then smiles, blinking too much, before he thanks Marjorie for the dance. She only has time to press his forearm before he separates himself and makes for the safety of the stage.

Most of the crowd watch as Charlie Thompson takes her hand in his. She feels his other hand, light against her shoulder blade. His face tenses as he strains to pick out the beat. Then they step into the mercy of darkness, his bad leg stammering out of time.

When he returns her to her table, Eleanor is talking to Jimmy Monaghan and she doesn't turn to acknowledge Marjorie.

Charlie Thompson hovers, his head bowed. 'Thank you for the dance, Marjorie. It was kind of you to put up with my two left feet.'

'Thank *you*, Mr Thompson!' She has to look away so the tears don't come.

He glances sternly at the rigid backs of Eleanor and Jimmy. 'I'm driving back to North Sydney now, in case you need a lift.'

She turns to the table and tries again. 'Eleanor?'

But Eleanor pretends not to hear, so Marjorie finds her clutch on the floor and tries to smile. 'Thank you. It *is* very late.'

Outside, the snow that was falling earlier has turned to sleet. As she waits on the sidewalk for Mr Thompson and his Buick, she watches two men approach, their unbuttoned coats flapping. Even in the wind, she can smell the liquor on them. When one slips on a patch of ice and almost hits the ground, she turns her face away. She pretends not to hear his friend mutter that the roads everywhere are 'as slick as a buttered-up bride'. But everything's fine because Mr Thompson's pulling up to the curb now. He's stepping outside to open her door, and as she bundles herself and her coat into the passenger seat, she surprises even herself. 'Cokeville.' She stares into her lap. 'Before we go back, Mr Thompson, would you show me Cokeville?'

His hand hovers over the gearbox. He has to clear his throat. 'Sure. Why the hell not?'

She smells it before she sees it: a stink of slag and human sewage. Under the angry candle of the steelworks tower, rows of dark bunkhouses and shacks materialise in the night.

Charlie Thompson turns off the engine, lights a cigarette and blows a plume of smoke into the night.

Something tightened in her chest. 'But Bill at the Foundry said these men are skilled labourers. I thought that's why they were asked to come all this way.'

'Yes.'

'I thought all the steelworkers and their families lived in the Ashby area.'

He offers her his cigarette. 'Not all.'

She shakes her head and pulls her coat tight. She suspects her hand will shake if she tries to smoke. Even here, now, she cares enough not to want to appear childish. Or hopeful. She doesn't want Mr Thompson to worry that she has misunderstood. He has only been kind and decent, and besides, what would she want with him? He's almost twice her age. Yet, here at the edge of Cokeville, a strange familiarity settles into the silence between them until Charlie finally rubs the windshield clear of the mist of their breath. 'It's after midnight, Marjorie.'

'Of course. I'm keeping you, and my mother will be waiting up.'

'Not to mention the fact that you'll get an earful from your big sister when she hears.' In the narrow space of the two-door Buick, he turns to her for the first time – and winks. 'I see her very . . . patient husband up at the track.'

She lets herself laugh.

'We'll take the harbour, shall we?' he says cheerfully. 'Make up a bit of lost time?'

She straightens in her seat, surfacing from the depths of her coat. 'Stan, Eleanor's brother, said the harbour is risky now.'

Charlie casts his cigarette into the night. 'I came that way. The ice was rock solid.' He grins. 'You don't think I'd play fast and loose with this baby, do you?' He thumps the steering wheel, then releases the handbrake.

A *gambler*, said Eleanor. 'Apparently, he's a *gambler*.' Of course, he'd have to be to offer her – a young, unmarried woman – a late-night lift home in the first place.

Not that she had to accept. Not that she had to ask him to detour to Cokeville. Not that he had to agree.

Maybe that makes them two of a kind, her and Charlie Thompson. She only knows that it's past midnight, the roads are bad – it will be a slow crawl back to North Sydney – and May will shame her come morning. She has no idea how she'll explain: about Walter, the lateness of the hour, about Mr Thompson, married and Protestant.

At Muggah's Creek, the new 1926 Buick Roadster glides on to the ice.

But even now, there's time. Will she say it?

Shall we turn back? Everyone says you shouldn't cross after the first of March.

No.

Because what's five days to twenty inches of ice, and hasn't it been snowing most of the night? Besides, it's just eight miles across. In a quarter of an hour, they'll be landing on the sandbar at Indian Beach.

She has never crossed by night before. The swollen sky bears down. In the wide, dark limbo of Sydney Harbour, the Buick's headlamps seem no brighter than a pair of jack-o'-lanterns.

Every year the Council says it will provide range lights and a few bush-marked courses, but the owners of the icebreakers protest. How will they clear the harbour's shipping lane with lights, markers and more traffic to circumnavigate?

As the car moves out across the frozen estuary, Charlie Thompson's hands are rigid on the wheel. Now and again, the car fantails, but he pulls it back into line and on they go.

She'll laugh on the other side. Perhaps she'll even have one of Mr Thompson's cigarettes or a swig from his flask to steady her nerves.

She would lay her head back and close her eyes – she's so tired now – but cold air blasts through the windows. Mr Thompson says they have to stay open so the windshield doesn't fog up.

And suddenly, for no reason, she remembers the old Micmac woman who came to the door selling baskets. Her black hair was shot through with silver, and she wore it loose on her shoulders. It dripped with snow and the woman's cheeks were wet. 'I'm sorry,' she said solemnly, taking Marjorie's mother's thin hand in her own. 'I am sorry about your three daughters.'

How did she know?

But 'No,' said Marjorie, rushing to her mother's aid, clarifying, taking back her mother's hand: 'My mother has lost two daughters and the son of the house. Two daughters. Three children. But thank you for your condolences.'

How sick she'd felt once the door was shut. The woman had done nothing wrong, and they should have bought her baskets.

Marjorie shakes herself. They are almost clear of the estuary. Another ten minutes and they'll be on terra firma. She tries to brighten. 'All things considered,' she says, turning to Charlie Thompson, 'I enjoyed myself tonight.'

He laughs, relieved to have conversation. 'I haven't danced so much in years!'

'You danced half of one dance!'

'Exactly. My wife will never believe it.'

She doesn't look at him as she says it. 'You'll tell your wife then?'

He leans forward, mopping the windshield with his sleeve. 'Haven't decided yet. I have a policy, you might say. Why worry today about that which you can put off till tomorrow?'

She nods, as if his answer is of no consequence to her.

'Which means,' he says, winking again, 'I'll think about it tomorrow when I'm sitting in church.'

'Where you can calmly postpone the question till another day!'

'Bullseye.'

She settles back into her seat, laughing. She recalls again the easy sway of her hips as she danced, and Walter's firm arm leading, and Mr Thompson bending over her, tall, close and protective. There's a tune stuck in her head, one of the big jazz numbers of the night. What was it called? The windshield wipers are going, they're lulling her to sleep, and it's only when Charlie Thompson looks over and catches her eye that she realises she's been humming the tune aloud. Her throat and cheeks go hot, but there's no need for blushes. He's singing. *Mr Thompson* is singing. Eleanor would never believe it. He's stringing together one line after the other, and it's all coming back: the deep, from-the-belly rhythm, the spell of the words, the stream in the moonlight, the honey who'll be gone by dawn. 'Tonight You Belong to Me'. That's the one. Charlie Thompson has a fine voice, she thinks to herself, when the car goes through the ice.

Her stomach drops; her spine goes rigid. The hole in the harbour opens like a black mouth. The Buick tips – her hands can't find the handle – and suddenly, unfathomably, the car is gripped in jaws of ice.

The headlamps are out, and she can't tell if the space above her is the window that faces up or down. His or hers. There's no top, no bottom, no floor, no roof, no ocean bed, no blind hole above. *Mr Thompson?* Through the open window, water and ice are rushing across her lap – *My coat, my new coat* – and her mind can't catch up.

I tell myself this.

She feels his hand grabbing at her shoulder – Thank God, she thinks, thank God. He's hauling her up by the wide collar of her coat. She's pushing off from the passenger door with her feet, gulping air. He's going ahead, showing her the way to the surface. She's grabbing hold of the hollow block of his shoe. Or is that the window frame? And is that his voice calling or the groaning of steel against ice?

The car shifts again, a wave churns through, the world rolls and—

No.

The car falls, juddering through ice. Down and down. *Mr Thompson!*

But he's nowhere.

Such darkness. Such cold. Like she has never known.

Her coat clings, sodden. Heavy. Unimaginably heavy.

A dead animal weight.

And the Micmac woman is beside her in the footwell – *Sssh now, quiet* – as the car sinks to the bottom of the estuary.

In the article in the *Herald* entitled 'Saturday Night's Tragedy', she will remain nameless. A 'young lady'. It is a kindness perhaps.

There will be no obituary. No public wake. No stews, loaves or cakes delivered to the door. No crowd of mourners, warm and close in the kitchen.

Only talk.

Her funeral will be attended by just four, her sisters May, Laura, Alice and Ignace. As the mass is said, her mother will close herself in 'Ethel's room' and draw the drapes.

In the years and generations to come, children will be named for her siblings, Ethel, Kathleen and Murray.

As for Charlie Thompson, he will never be able to get a song out of his head, and in the black waters of sleep, it will slow into a dirge and boom between his ears. 'Tonight you belong to me.'

Sometimes, I tell people about my great-aunt who went under the ice.

Solo, A Cappella

Everywhere in Tottenham that evening, you could smell summer: mown grass from the football ground, the stink of hot tarmac, rubbish baking in the bins and the whiff off the WD-40 cans our yutes was huffing on the estates. But up at the Pond, *man*, the air smelled good: all watery green and sweet with long grass. The dragonflies were zupping, and high above them, the bats were zigzagging in and out of the bat-boxes. Me and Valentine, we sat there, listenin' to the males singing for mates – whistlin' and wantin' – as the sun dropped from the sky.

Valentine said they was 'pipistrelles'. She'd been on a nature walk with her class along ditches that used to be river. I said, *pipistrelles*, lah-dee-dah, and pulled her close, so close I could smell the bubble-gum taste of her lip gloss and the warmth of her skin.

She said a certain kind up there at the Pond was rare, a *soprano* pipistrelle, which was different than the *common* pipistrelle. I said, well, if bats was human, she'd be the soprano and I'd be the common, and *she* said that if I'd shut my mouth she might even be able to hear the pips what bats bounce off everything. So I went quiet and she went still, and her face lit up. Then she nodded like an old African wise woman, and I said, 'I can't hear nothing,' and she said that's because mostly only teen-aged girls can hear those pips.

'Special feelers,' she said, wiggling the ear lobe I longed to kiss.

But maybe that's where she was wrong, cos later on, she didn't feel *no* trouble coming. Or maybe she did, but she did what she did anyway.

Back in April, I was eighteen and she was still fifteen when I sidled into her booth at the McDonald's on the High Road, nervous behind my smile. She was with her friend Cherelle, but neither told me to bounce. Valentine only corrected me, saying her name was 'Valenteen', because it was French, and not Valenteyene. Just the fact that she wanted me to know how to say her name made me high with hope. It didn't matter that she hardly looked up from her McNuggets. So I was mannerly to Cherelle, but I talked and whistled and wanted for Valentine. My thoughts zupped all over my head as I looked at her eyes – downturned and fluted – and the bright heart of her face.

Her family were Congolese, which meant she sounded French and African both when she spoke English. Maybe that's why she didn't open her mouth much, except when she had to, like at Community Choir practice on Tuesday nights. Mostly it was white old people in the choir but she said she didn't mind, and I knew she didn't mind because of that voice on her. Pure like summer rain. Once she sang for me up at the Pond – from a religious song called 'Gloria' – and I said 'You nailed that,' but I knew my words weren't good enough for that voice of hers rising high over the Pond, making even the bats go still. She said she'd been practising for months and was going to sing solo, a cappella. Her piece was called the 'Domine Deus' which meant, she said, 'Lord God'.

'Lord *God!*' I shouted to the sky, and we both grinned.

She was opposite like that: shy but with a big voice when she was brave enough to use it. Mostly, it was good I could talk for two. I think she liked my talking. Talking was how I survived the jungle that is the shop floor of H&M where I work three days a week – or maybe never again if the CCTV was eyeballing me as I ducked out of Superdrug on Saturday night.

My father was once the driver for a big politician in Ghana. But when things started to go wrong for the Big-Wig, most of his men were stuffed into barrels that had been shot through till they were more like sieves. Then they was put to sea. Now my dad drives buses by day and works at Pizza Hut by night. When I'm on his bus and see gangs of boys as young as twelve flickin' the knives and vexin' and callin' him 'old man', my heart jams. Once I strode to the front of the bus to take on the little evils, but through the glass my father said, *John, don't be an idiot*, and he nodded at me hard to sit down. What he meant was, *Isn't one loss in the family enough for you?* My mother lasted two years after her stroke. She was forty-five, too young to die, everyone says in England, but old enough in Ghana.

I told Valentine all this one night at the Pond, but she never gabbed about her own fam. I only know they'd been on The Farm two years – that's the Broadwater Farm Estate to you and the people at the Council. I got the vibe they was illegal; that Valentine worried that if she said the wrong thing to the wrong person, they'd be sent back to the Congo in a puff of smoke.

Maybe she was right. Maybe they was. Or maybe her family decided fast to move on, out of Tottenham, after Saturday night.

All I know is, she's nowhere, and now, I'm not the only one wondering. Cos there's a video, supposedly of a 'sixteen-year-old African girl', posted on YouTube on Saturday night where you can't hardly see nothing, but, *man*, it went viral. There was an old woman eyewitness and a man watching from a church where he'd run for cover. And there are reporters trying to find this girl. And community folk scratching their heads. And the police hoping to hell she never was real.

But Valentine was real in my arms that night as the sun set and the smog turned orange over Tottenham. I found a stone in the grass that was pinkish and sort of in the shape of a heart, so I gave it to her, like it was a gift from the Pond and me both, and she turned it over in her hands while the bats whooshed above us. Then I smiled, waggling my eyebrows. I was well switched, but she said, 'Nuh-uh, not without a condom,' and I remembered my mother. She was laughing through that stroke-slumped smile of hers, passing me my first box of Durex and slurring, 'Don't you dare forget.'

We had a plan. I said I'd get myself to Superdrug. Valentine said she'd go home, chat with her parents, then slip out her window; it was the only advantage to a ground-floor apartment on The Farm. Valentine was good at popping the grille.

We said we'd meet at nine at the usual place, the old covered well on the High Road. Sometimes we'd just stand there and try to imagine what Tottenham must have been like when it was a village, and what The

Farm must have been like when it was a farm, with cows at the Pond. We never could.

Most of the rest you know already. You saw it on your iPod Touch or in HD on your plasma. Maybe you watched it on YouTube on your day off.

There must have been a thousand yutes and by the time I got there, looking for Valentine, they was already chanting loud: 'Whose streets? Our streets!' Then the Feds pushed up at the barricades near McDonald's. Up close, they say their eyes was wide. Sometimes you wouldn't change places for the world.

But soon the snatch-squads rolled up with their riot gear and their horses and their Alsatians ready to chew the legs off anything standin' still. So out came the ballies, the bottles, the bats, bars and bricks. Out came the fireworks, the hammers and the petrol cans. The barricades were set on fire. Blue lights strobed. Searchlights slashed the sky, and the helicopters over-head sounded like damnation. Boss cars – Mercs and Beemers – got wrecked. Petrol tanks went off like Christmas crackers.

'Dead the fires! Dead the fires!' I pinged that off as night fell, but two police cars was already shells, and by eleven, the double-decker on my father's route was flamin' high into the night with its automated lady saying: 'This bus is under attack. Please dial 999. This bus is under attack . . .' Until she couldn't take the heat no longer.

Then Aldi got torched and Carpetright too, with all those people burned out of their flats, and harassed on their way out, which was twisted. I don't know *no one* who thinks any different.

The night was like some kind of video game. For once, the yutes were bigger than the police. They were fightin' like soldiers at those barricades, givin' it large. They were the ones doin' the stoppin' and searchin'. They had the Feds under manners. On lock. On smash. Running away. Gangs from all over London put down their beef that night to come together. They had ransack of the place – and it was all being broadcast live, in real-time, on BlackBerry. 'Let's eat together,' they said. 'Eat' means get. Let's get stuff together. People was part of something. For once, they wasn't nothing.

Me, I just kept walkin' the High Road, looking for Valentine. At the barricades, the front half was holding the Feds back so the back half could rip. *Man*, they had trollies and suitcases and wheelie bins. For a long, stupid while, I tried shouting that the looting wasn't helping nothin', but I might as well have been singing 'The Wheels on the Bus'.

I saw kids as young as ten. I saw one take a golf club to the T-Mobile window. I saw an old geezer with boxes of trainers stacked high in his arms. I saw people dishing out lottery tickets and cigarettes like they was sweets. 'Here comes the Revolution!' one Paki guy was shouting. Hundreds was walking round with the Nike Air Forces, the G-Star jeans, the plasmas, the iPhone 4s, the iPads and stereos. They was trying on clothes in the front gardens of strangers. I saw women walking away with nappies, soap powder and bags of rice. I watched a skinny guy steal protein drinks from a health food place, while across the street, an old posh lady was waving a bottle of Lambrusco.

I saw old and young, African and Caribbean, White and Asian working together to push up steel shutters. It was harmony for those guys, sweet and true.

I never saw Valentine. I told myself she must have heard what was going down before she left the apartment. I didn't check my phone because she didn't have a phone. Her parents couldn't afford even a pay-as-you-go.

There was a fog of smoke all night. People were making jokes, like about not burning down McDonald's cos they might need a burger later; cos all this ninja stuff could put a hunger on. Me, I thought, who will care about anyone rippin' one box of Durex? I was still longing for Valentine, and the window at Superdrug was all smashed in. If Saturday was totalled, there was still Sunday at the Pond in the twilight in the long grass. There was still most of August.

Girls were in there before me, taking shampoo, false eyelashes and pocketfuls of lip gloss. Hope is cheaper than you think. My eyes met theirs and we all laughed like we was old friends.

The riot that night weren't wrong and it weren't right either. It's just what happens when a man from The Farm is shot dead and no one knows why, and the Feds close ranks and won't talk till they are made to talk, and people have been there before – literally at the door of that station waiting and asking for answers that aren't in the leaflets they're being told to read.

Sometimes, you just want to *breathe*. Sometimes you want to know nothing. You want to be pure and clean, like Valentine's voice singing that 'Lord God' song up at the Pond. That night I saw a Fed dragged off into a back alley by maybe six yutes, each with a torn-off plank. I saw nails glinting.

It took the Feds till midnight to grab back just 200 metres of the High Road, and by four, the riot had moved to the Station. I've been in there myself and knuckled and that, and when everyone was putting in their windows, I personally didn't feel no inclination to stop nobody.

Then, as the night started to thin towards day, I checked my BlackBerry and found the threads about the girl. One said she was ten years old. Another said she was pregnant. But most everyone agreed: it was a sixteen-year-old African girl what turned the protest into a riot.

Later I pieced some of it together. While she was up at the Pond with me that Saturday, her parents was doin' the march from The Farm to the Station – which was totally brave if they was illegal. Valentine's mum and little sister was up at the front with maybe fifty other women. The women was leading, with their children, their buggies and their sad banners. It was a way of saying to the Feds, *This is a peaceful protest*. Behind them was their men, and behind *them*, was the yutes of The Farm.

Five hours passed and the Chief Superintendent never appeared.

Cherelle told me that Valentine walked from The Farm to the High Road to find out what was taking her parents so long. Her little sister would have been hot and hungry, and her mother, tired on her feet.

At half eight, the women said they couldn't wait no more. The children had to be put to bed. Their men followed, defeat in their shoulders. Only the yutes stayed, humming like wasps.

Then out came the first of the Feds. That's when the girl appeared, or so they say. They say she walked up to one Fed and, in a clear voice, much bigger than she was, told him that people needed answers. He told her to get home if she knew what was good for her. They say she threw a leaflet at him. A few others came, looked down and laughed. Or they did until she backed up, reached into her pocket and threw a stone.

It bounced off a bullet-proof.

Lord God.

Them who was there say fifteen of them circled her. They licked at her legs with their truncheons. One raised his fist. She was bleeding, and people started screaming into the night. Which is when word was pinged off on BlackBerry, and London came to Tottenham.

For days after, I went to The Farm, first in the heat, then in the rain, trying to figure out even which high-rise was hers. But people don't want to talk after a night like that, not even to a black guy from the manor. By the time I found Cherelle and got the address, Valentine and her family was gone.

Fact is, I don't know what's true and what's story. I only know about Valentine up at the Pond, and the bats whistlin' and wantin', and her voice so pure it made a stillness of everything.

Sixteen-year-old African girl. Solo, a cappella.

The Heart of Denis Noble

As Denis Noble, Professor of Cardiovascular Physiology, succumbs to the opioids – a meandering river from the IV drip – he is informed his heart is on its way. In twenty, perhaps thirty minutes' time, the Cessna air ambulance will land in the bright, crystalline light of December, on the small landing-strip behind the Radcliffe Hospital.

A bearded jaw appears over him. From this angle, the mouth is oddly labial. Does he understand? Professor Noble nods from the other side of the ventilation mask. He would join in the team chat but the mask prevents it, and in any case, he must lie still so the nurse can shave the few hairs that remain on his chest.

He can rest easy, someone assures him. His heart is beating well at 40,000 feet, out of range of all turbulence. 'We need your research, Professor,' another voice jokes from behind the ECG monitor. 'We're taking no chances!'

Which isn't to say that the whole thing isn't a terrible gamble.

The nurse has traded the shaver for a pair of nail-clippers. She sets to work on the nails of his right hand, his plucking hand. Is that necessary? he wants to ask. It will take him some time to grow them back, assuming of course he still has 'time'. As she slips the pulse oxime-ter over his index finger, he wonders if Joshua will show any interest at all in the classical guitar he is destined to inherit, possibly any day now. According to his mother, Josh is into electronica and urban soul.

A second nurse bends and whispers in his ear like a lover. 'Now all you have to do is relax, Denis. We've got everything covered.' Her breath is warm. Her breast is near. He can imagine the gloss of her lips. He wishes she would stay by his ear for ever. 'We'll have you feel-ing like yourself again before you know it.'

He feels he might be sick.

Then his choice of pre-op music – the second move-ment of Schubert's Piano Trio in E-flat major – seems to flow, sweet and grave, from her mouth into his ear, and once more he can see past the red and golden treetops of Gordon Square to his attic room of half a century ago. A recording of the Schubert is rising through the floor-boards, and the girl beside him in his narrow student bed is warm; her lips brush the lobe of his ear; her voice alone, the whispered current of it, is enough to arouse him. But when her fingers find him beneath the sheet, they surprise him with a catheter, and he has to shut his eyes against the tears, against the absurdity of age.

The heart of Denis Noble beat for the first time on the 5th of March 1936 in the body of Ethel Noble as she stitched a breast pocket to a drape-cut suit in an upstairs room at Wilson & Jeffries, the tailoring house where she first met her husband George, a trainee cutter, across a flashing length of gold silk lining.

As she pierced the wool with her basting needle, she remembered George's tender, awkward kiss to her collarbone that morning, and, as if in reply, Denis's heart, a mere tube at this point, beat its first of more than two billion utterances – da dum. Unknown to Ethel, she was twenty-one days pregnant. Her thread dangled briefly in mid-air.

Soon, the tube that was Denis Noble's heart, a delicate scrap of mesoderm, would push towards life. In the dark of Ethel, it would twist and grope, looping blindly back upon itself. In this unfolding, intra-uterine drama, Denis Noble – a dangling button on the thread of life – would begin to take shape, to hold fast. He would inherit George's high forehead and Ethel's bright almond-shaped eyes. His hands would be small but unusually dexterous. A birthmark would stamp itself on his left hip. But inasmuch as he was flesh, blood and bone, he was also, deep within Ethel, a living stream of sound and sensation, a delicate flux of stimuli, the influence of which eluded all known measure, then as now.

He was the cloth smoothed beneath Ethel's cool palm, and the pumping of her foot on the pedal of the Singer machine. He was the hiss of her iron over the sleeve press and the clink of brass pattern-weights in her apron pocket. He was the soft spring light through the open window, the warmth of it bathing her face, and the serotonin surging in her synapses at the sight of a magnolia tree in flower. He was the manifold sound-waves of passers-by: of motor cars hooting, of old men hocking and spitting, and of delivery boys teetering down Savile Row under bolts of cloth bigger than they were. Indeed it is impossible to say where Denis stopped and the world began.

★

Only on a clear, cloudless night in November 1940 did the world seem to unstitch itself from the small boy he was and separate into something strange, something other. Denis opened his eyes to the darkness. His mother was scooping him from his bed and running down the stairs so fast, his head bumped up and down against her shoulder.

Downstairs, his father wasn't in his armchair with the newspaper on his lap, but on the sitting-room floor cutting cloth by the light of a torch. Why was Father camping indoors? 'Let's sing a song,' his mother whispered, but she forgot to tell him which song to sing.

The kitchen was a dark place and no, it wasn't time for eggs and soldiers, not yet, she shooshed, and even as she spoke, she was depositing him beneath the table next to the fat yellow bundle that was his sister, and stretching out beside him, even though her feet in their court shoes stuck out the end. 'There, there,' she said as she pulled them both to her. Then they turned their ears towards a sky they couldn't see and listened to the planes that droned like angry bees in the jar of the south London night.

When the bang came, the floor shuddered beneath them and plaster fell in lumps from the ceiling. His father rushed in from the sitting room, pins still gripped between his lips. Before his mother had finished thanking God, Denis felt his legs propel him, without permission, not even his own, to the window to look. Beneath a corner of the blackout curtain, at the bottom of the garden, flames were leaping. 'Fire!' he shouted, but his father shouted louder, nearly swallowing his pins – 'GET AWAY from the window!' – and plucked him into the air.

They owed their lives, his mother would later tell Mrs West next door, to a cabinet minister's suit. Their Anderson Shelter, where they would have been huddled were it not for the demands of bespoke design, had taken a direct hit.

The shelter was flattened and beside it, Denis's father's shed had caught fire. That night, George and a dicky stirrup-pump waged a losing battle against the flames until neighbours joined in with rugs, hoses and buckets of sand. Denis stood behind his mother's hip at the open door. His baby sister howled from her Moses basket. Smoke gusted as he watched his new red wagon melt in the heat. Ethel smiled down at him, squeezing his hand, and it seemed very odd because his mother shook as much as she smiled and she smiled as much as she shook.

As Denis beheld his mother – her eyes wet with tears, her hair unpinned, her arms goose-pimpled – he felt something radiate through his chest. It warmed him through. He felt very light. If his mother hadn't been wearing her heavy navy-blue court shoes, the two of them, he thought, might have floated off the doorstep into the night. At the same time, the feeling was an ache, a hole, a sore inside him. It made him feel heavy. It made it hard to breathe. Something in his chest seemed too big. As the tremor in his mother's arm travelled into his hand, up his arm, through his armpit and into his chest, he felt for the first time the mysterious life of the heart.

He had of course been briefed in the weeks prior to surgery. His consultant, Mr Bonham, had sat at his desk, his chins doubling with the gravity of the situation, as he reviewed Denis's notes. The tests had been incon-clusive but the 'rather urgent' need for transplantation remained clear.

Naturally he would, Mr Bonham said, be familiar with the procedure. An incision in the ribcage. The removal of the pericardium – 'a slippery business, but straight-forward enough'. Denis's heart would be emptied, and the aorta clamped prior to excision. 'Routine.' The chest cavity would be cleared, though the biatrial cuff would be left in place. Then the new heart would be 'unveiled – *voila!*', and the aorta engrafted, followed by the pulmonary artery.

Mr Bonham was widely reputed to be the last eccen-tric standing in the NHS, but he was reassuringly expert. Most grafts, Mr Bonham noted, recovered normal ventricular function without intervention. There were risks, of course: bleeding, RV failure, bradyarrhythmias, conduction abnormalities, sudden death.

'But onward, what!' he boomed, and Denis would have eagerly agreed had not a blush climbed up Mr Bonham's throat as he closed Denis's file.

The allegro now. The third movement of the Piano Trio – *faster, faster* – but the Schubert is receding, and as Denis surfaces from sleep, he realises he's being whisked down the wide, blanched corridors of the Heart Unit. His trolley is a precision vehicle. It glides. It shunts around corners. There's no time to waste – the heart must be fresh – and he wonders if he has missed his stop. Kentish Town. Archway. Highgate. East Finchley. The names of the stations flicker past like clues in a dream to a year he cannot quite summon. Tunnel after tunnel. He mustn't nod off again, mustn't miss the stop,

but the carriage is swaying and rocking, it's only quarter past five in the morning and it's hard to resist the
ramshackle lullaby of the Northern Line.

West Finchley. Woodside Park.

1960.

That's the one.

It's 1960, but no one, it seems, has told the good
people of Totteridge. Each time he steps on to the platform at the quaint, well-swept station, he feels as if he
has been catapulted back in time.

The slaughterhouse is a fifteen-minute walk along
a B-road, and Denis is typically the first customer of
the day. He feels underdressed next to the workers in
their whites, their hard hats, their metal aprons and
their steel-toed wellies. They stare, collectively, at his
loafers.

Slaughter-men aren't talkers by nature, but nevertheless, over the months, Denis has come to know each
by name. Front of house, there's Alf the Shackler, Frank
the Knocker, Jimmy the Sticker, Marty the Plucker
and Mike the Splitter. Frank tells him how, years ago,
a sledgehammer saw him through the day's routine,
but now it's a pneumatic gun and a bolt straight to
the brain; a few hundred shots a day, which means he
has to wear goggles, 'cos of all the grey matter flying'.
He's worried he's developing 'trigger-finger', and he
removes his plastic glove so Denis can see for himself
'the finger what won't uncurl'.

Alf is brawny but soft-spoken with kind, almost
womanly eyes. Every morning on the quiet, he tosses
Denis a pair of wellies to spare his shoes. No one
mentions the stink of the place, a sharp kick to the
lungs of old blood, manure and offal. The breeze-block

walls exhale it and the floor reeks of it, even though the place is mopped down like a temple every night.

Jimmy is too handsome for a slaughterhouse, all dirty blond curls and American teeth, but he doesn't know it because he's a farm boy who's never been farther than East Finchley. Marty, on the other hand, was at Dunkirk. He has a neck like a battering ram and a lump of shrapnel in his head. Every day, at the close of business, he brings his knife home with him on the passenger seat of his Morris Mini Minor. He explains to Denis that he spends a solid hour each night sharpening and sanding the blade to make sure it's smooth with no pits. 'An' 'e wonders,' bellows Mike, 'why 'e can't get a bird!'

Denis pays £4 for two hearts a day, a sum that left him stammering with polite confusion on his first visit. At Wilson & Jeffries, his father earns £20 per week.

Admittedly, they bend the rules for him. Frank 'knocks' the first sheep as usual. Alf shackles and hoists. But Jimmy, who grasps his sticking knife – Jimmy, the youngest, who's always keen, literally, to 'get stuck in' – doesn't get to slit the throat and drain the animal. When Denis visits, there's a different running order. Jimmy steps aside, and Marty cuts straight into the chest and scoops out 'the pluck'. The blood gushes. The heart and lungs steam in Marty's hands. The others tut-tut like old women at the sight of the spoiled hide, but Marty is butchery in motion. He casts the lungs down a chute, passes the warm heart to Denis, rolls the stabbed sheep down the line to Mike the Splitter, shouts, 'Chop, chop, ha ha' at Mike and waits like a veteran for Alf to roll the second sheep his way.

Often Denis doesn't wait to get back to the lab. He pulls a large pair of scissors from his holdall, grips the heart at arm's length, cuts open the meaty ventricles, checks to ensure the Purkinje fibres are still intact, then pours a steady stream of Tyrode solution over and into the heart. When the blood is washed clear, he plops the heart into his Thermos and waits for the next heart as the gutter in the floor fills with blood. The Tyrode solution, which mimics the sugar and salts of blood, is a simple but strange elixir. Denis still can't help but take a schoolboy sort of pleasure in its magic. There in his Thermos, at the core of today's open heart, the Purkinje fibres have started to beat again. Very occasionally, a whole ventricle comes to life. On those occasions, he lets Jimmy hold the disembodied heart as if it is a wounded bird fluttering between his palms.

Then the Northern Line flickers past in reverse until Euston Station reappears, where Denis hops out and jogs – Thermos and scissors clanging in the holdall – down Gower Street, past the main quad, through the Anatomy entrance, up the grand century-old staircase to the second floor and into the empty lab before the clock on the wall strikes seven.

In the hush of the Radcliffe's principal operating theatre, beside the anaesthetised, intubated body of Denis Noble, Mr Bonham assesses the donor heart for a final time.

The epicardial surface is smooth and glistening. The quantity of fat is negligible. The lumen of the coronary artery is large, without any visible narrowing. The heart is still young, after all; sadly, just seventeen years old, though, in keeping with protocol, he has revealed nothing of the donor identity to the patient, and Professor Noble knows better than to ask.

Preoperative monitoring has confirmed strong wall motion, excellent valve function, good conduction and regular heart rhythm.

It's a ticklish business at the best of times, he reminds his team, but yes, he is ready to proceed.

In the lab of the Anatomy Building, Denis pins out the heart like a valentine. The buried trove, the day's booty, is nestled at the core; next to the red flesh of the ventricle, the Purkinje network is a skein of delicate yellow fibres. They gleam like the bundles of pearl cotton his mother used to keep in her embroidery basket.

Locating them is one thing. Getting them is another. It is tricky work to lift them free; trickier still to cut away sections without destroying them. He needs a good eye, a small pair of surgical scissors and the steady cutting hand he inherited, he likes to think, from his father. If impatience gets the better of him, if his scissors slip, it will be a waste of a fresh and costly heart. Beyond the lab door, an undergrad class thunders down the staircase. Outside, through the thin Victorian-glass panes, Roy Orbison croons 'Only the Lonely' on a transistor radio.

He boils water on the Bunsen burner someone pinched from the chemistry lab. The instant coffee is on the shelf with the bell jars. He pours, using his sleeve as a mitt, and, in the absence of a spoon, uses the pencil that's always tucked behind his ear.

At the vast chapel-arch of a window, he can just see the treetops of Gordon Square, burnished with autumn, and far below, the gardeners raking leaves and lifting bulbs. Beyond it, from this height, he can see as far as Tavistock Square, though the old copper beech stands between him and a view of his own attic window at the top of Connaught Hall.

He tries not to think about Ella, whom he hopes to find, several hours from now, on the other side of that window, in his room – i.e. his bed – where they have agreed to meet to 'compare the findings' of their respective days. Ella, a literature student, has been coolly bluffing her way into the Press Box at the Old Bailey this week. For his part, he'd never heard of the infamous novel until the headlines got hold of it, but Ella is gripped, and even the sound of her voice in his ear fills him with a desire worthy of the finest dirty book.

He fills the first micropipette with potassium chloride, inserts the silver thread-wire and connects it to the valve on his home-made amp. Soon, Antony and Günter, his undergrad assistants, will shuffle in for duty. He'll post Antony, with the camera and a stockpile of film, at the oscilloscope's screen. Günter will take to the darkroom next to the lab, and emerge pale and blinking at the end of the day.

He prepares a slide, sets up the Zeiss, switches on its light and swivels the lens into place. The view is good. His wrist is steady, which means every impulse from the heart, every rapid-fire excitation, should travel up the pipette through the thread-wire and into the valve of the amplifier. The oscilloscope will 'listen' to the amp. Fleeting waves of voltage will rise and fall across its screen, and Antony will snap away on the Nikon, capturing every fluctuation, every trace. Günter, for his part, has already removed himself like a penitent to the darkroom. There, if all goes well, he'll capture the divine spark of life on Kodak paper, over and over again.

In time, they'll convert the electrical ephemera of the day into scrolling graphs; they'll chart the unfolding peaks and troughs; they'll watch on paper the ineffable currents that compel the heart to life.

'Tell me,' says Ella, 'about the excitable cells. I like those.' Their heads share one pillow. Schubert's piano trio is rising through the floorboards. A cello student he has yet to meet lives below.

'I'll give you excitable.' He pinches her buttock. She bites the end of his nose. Through the crack of open window, they can smell trampled leaves, wet pavement and frost-bitten earth. In the night above the attic window, the stars throb.

She sighs luxuriously and shifts, so that Denis has to grip the mattress of the narrow single bed. 'Excuse me, but I'm about to go over the edge.'

'Of the bed or your mental health? Have you found those canals yet?'

'Channels.'

'Yes. Plutonium channels.'

'Potassium.'

'What?'

'Potassium channels.' He rolls her towards him and kisses her nipple. He is someone different with her.

'What do you do with these potassium channels?'

He surfaces from her cleavage. 'I map their electrical activity. I demonstrate the movement of ions – electrically charged particles – through cell membranes.' At the mattress edge, he gets hold of her hip.

'Why aren't you more pleased?'

'I am. Now tell me about your day.'

'I thought you said those channels of yours were *the* challenges.'

'Yes. It's going well. Ta.' He throws back the eider-down, springs to his feet and rifles through her shoulder bag for her notebook. 'Is it in here?'

'Is what?'

'Your notebook.'

'A man's testicles are never at their best as he bends.'

He waves the notebook. 'Did the Wigs put on a good show today?'

She folds her arms across the eiderdown. 'I'm not telling you until you tell me about your potassium what-nots.'

'Channels.' Across the room, he flips through the notebook. 'They're simply passages or pores in the cell membrane that allow a mass of charged ions to be shunted into the cell – or out of it again if there's an excess.'

She smooths her hair and sighs. 'If it's all so matter of fact, why are you bothering?'

He returns, kisses the top of her head and negotiates his way back into the bed. 'My supervisor put me on the case, and, like I say, all's well. I'm getting the results, rather more quickly than I expected, so I'm pleased. Because in truth, I would have looked a little silly if I hadn't found them. They're already known to exist in muscle cells, and the heart is only another muscle after all.'

'Only another muscle?'

'Yes.' He passes her the notebook.

'But this is something that has you running through Bloomsbury in the middle of the night for a date with a computer.'

He kisses her shoulder. 'The computer isn't nearly so amiable as you.'

'Denis Noble, are you doing important work or aren't you?'

'I have a dissertation to produce.'

She frowns. 'Never be, you know . . . matter of fact. Men who aren't curious bore me. Tell me what you will discover next.' She divests him of his half of the eiderdown.

'If I know, it won't be a discovery.'

'Perhaps it isn't an "it",' she muses. 'Have you thought of that?'

'When is an "it" not an "it"?'

'I'm not sure,' she says, and she wraps herself up like the Queen of Sheba. The eiderdown crackles with static, and her fine, shiny hair flies away in the light of the desk lamp. 'A book, for example, is not an "it".'

'Of course it's an "it". It's an object, a thing. Ask any girl in her deportment class, as she walks about with one on her head.'

'All right. A *story* is not an "it". It's a living thing.'

He smiles beseechingly. 'Perhaps we should save the metaphysics for after?'

'Every part of a great story "contains" every other part. Every small part anticipates the whole. Nothing can be passive or static. Not if it's great and . . . true to life. Nothing is just a part. Not really. Because the whole cannot be divided. That's what a real creation is. It has its own unity.' She pauses to examine the birthmark on his hip, a new discovery. 'The heart is, I suspect, a great creation, so the same rule will apply.'

'Which *rule* might that be?' He loves listening to her, even if he has no choice but to mock her, gently.

'The same principle then.'

He raises an eyebrow.

She adjusts her generous breasts. 'The principle of Eros. Eros is an attractive force. It binds the world; it makes connections. At best, it gives way to a sense of wholeness, a sense of the sacred even; at worst, it leads to fuzzy vision. Logos, your contender, particularises. It makes the elements of the world distinct. At best, it is illuminating; at worst, it is reductive. It cheapens. Both are vital. The balance is the thing. You need Eros, Denis. You're missing Eros.'

He taps her notebook. 'On that point, we agree wholeheartedly. I need to . . . connect.'

She studies him warily, then opens the spiral-bound stenographer's notebook. In the days before the trial, she taught herself shorthand in record time simply to capture, like any other putative member of the press, the banned passages of prose. She was determined to help carry their erotic charge into the world. 'T. S. Eliot was supposed to give evidence for the defence today, but apparently he sat in his taxi and couldn't bring himself to "do the deed".'

'Old men – impotent. Young men' – he smiles shyly – 'ready.' He opens her notebook to a random page of shorthand. The ink is purple.

'My little joke,' she says. 'A sense of humour is de rigueur in the Press Box.' She nestles into the pillow. He pats down her electric hair. 'From Chapter Ten,' she begins. '"Then with a quiver of exquisite pleasure he touched the warm soft body, and touched her navel for a moment in a kiss. And he had to come into her at once, to enter the peace on earth of her soft, quiescent body."'

'That gamekeeper chap doesn't hang about,' he says, laying his head against her breast and listening to the beat of her heart as she reads. Her voice enters him like a current and radiates through him until he feels himself hum with it, as if he is the body of a violin or cello that exists only to amplify her voice. He suspects he is not in love with her – and that is really just as well – but it occurs to him that he has never known such sweetness, such delight. He tries to stay in the moment, to loiter in the beats between the words she reads, between the breaths she takes. He runs his hand over the bell of her hip and tries not to think that in just four hours he will set off into the darkened streets of Bloomsbury, descend a set of basement steps and begin his night shift in the company of the only computer in London that is powerful enough to crunch his milliseconds of data into readable equations.

As a lowly biologist, an ostensible lightweight among the physicists and computer chaps, he has been allocated the least enviable slot on the computer, from two till four a.m. By five, he'll be on the Northern Line again, heading for the slaughterhouse.

Ella half wakes as he leaves.

'Go back to sleep,' he whispers, grabbing his jacket and the holdall.

She sits up in bed, blinking in the light of the lamp which he has turned to the wall. 'Are you going now?'

'Yes.' He smiles, glancing at her, finds his wallet and checks he has enough cash for the hearts of the day. 'Bye, then.'

'Goodbye, Denis,' she says softly.

'Sweet dreams,' he says.

But she doesn't stretch and settle back under the eiderdown. She remains upright and naked, even though the room is so cold, their breath has turned to frost on the inside of the window. He wonders if there isn't something odd in her expression. He hovers for a moment before deciding it is either a shadow from the lamp or the residue of a dream. Whatever the case, he can't be late for his shift. If he is, the porter won't be there to let him in.

He switches off the lamp.

In his later years, Denis Noble has allowed himself to wonder, privately, about the physiology of love. He has loved – with gratitude and frustration – parents, siblings, a spouse and two children. What, he asks himself, is love if not a force within? And what is a force within if not something *lived through* the body? Nevertheless, as Emeritus Professor of Cardiovascular Physiology, he has to admit he knows little more about love than he did on the night he fell in love with his mother; the night their shelter was bombed; the night he felt with utter certainty the strange life of the heart in his chest.

Before 1960 drew to a close, he would – like hundreds of thousands of other liberated readers – buy the banned book and try to understand it as Ella had understood it. Later still in life, he would dedicate himself to the music and poetry of the Occitan troubadours. He would read and reread the ancient sacred-sexual texts of the Far East. He would learn, almost by heart, St Teresa's account of her vision of the loving seraph: '*I saw in his hands a long spear of gold . . . He appeared to me to be thrusting it at times into my heart . . .*' The Bernini sculpture of her in Rome was a favourite.

But *what*, he wanted to ask St Teresa, could the heart, that feat of flesh, blood and voltage, have to do with love? *Where*, he'd like to know, is love?

★

On the train to Totteridge, he can still smell the citrus of Ella's perfume on his hands, in spite of the punched paper-tape offerings he's been feeding to the computer through the night. He only left its subterranean den an hour ago.

He is allowed 'to live' and to sleep from seven each evening to half past one the next morning, when his alarm wakes him for his shift in the computer unit. He closes the door on the darkness of Connaught Hall and sprints across Bloomsbury. After his shift, he travels from the Comp. Science basement to the Northern Line, from the Northern Line to the slaughterhouse, from the slaughterhouse to Euston and from Euston to the lab for his twelve-hour day.

He revels briefly in the thought of a pretty girl still asleep in his bed, a luxury he'd never, as a science student, dared hope to win. Through the smeared carriage windows, the darkness is thinning into a murky dawn. The Thermos jiggles in the holdall at his feet, the carriage door rattles and clangs, and his head falls back.

Up ahead, Ella is standing naked and grand on a bright woodland path in Tavistock Square. She doesn't seem to care that she can be seen by all the morning commuters and the students rushing past on their way to classes. She slips through the gate at the western end of the square and turns, closing it quickly. As he reaches it, he realises it is a kissing gate. She stands on the other side but refuses him her lips. 'Gates open,' she says tenderly, '*and they close.*' He tries to go through but she shakes her head. When he pulls on the gate, he gets an electric shock. 'Why are you surprised?' she says.

The dream returns to him only later as Marty is scooping the pluck from the first sheep on the line.

He feels again the force of the electric shock in the dream.

The gate was conductive.

It opened . . .

It *closed*.

He receives from Marty the first heart of the day. It's hot between his palms but he doesn't reach for his scissors. Deep within him, it's as if his own heart has been jump-started to life.

In the operating theatre, Mr Bonham and his team have been at work for three-and-a-half hours, when at last he gives the word. Professor Noble can be disconnected from the bypass machine. His pulse is strong. The new heart, declares Mr Bonham, 'is going great guns'.

Denis's dream of Ella at the gate means he can't finish at the slaughterhouse quickly enough. On the train back into town, he swears under his breath at the eternity of every stop. In the lab, the insertion of the micropipette has been hit and miss. Antony and Günter exchange looks. When they request a lunch break, he stares into the middle distance. When Günter complains that his hands are starting to burn from the fixatives, Denis looks up from the Zeiss, as if at a tourist who requires something of him in another language.

Finally, when the great window is a chapel arch of darkness and rain, he closes and locks the lab door behind him. There is nothing in his appearance to suggest anything other than a long day's work. No one he passes on the staircase of the Anatomy Building pauses to look. No one glances back, pricked by an intuition or an afterthought. He has forgotten his jacket, but the sight of a poorly dressed student is nothing to make anyone look twice.

Yet as he steps into the downpour of the night, every light is blazing in his head. In the dazzle of his own thoughts, he hardly sees where he's going but he's running, across Gordon Square and on towards Tavistock . . . He wants to shout the news to the winos who shelter from the rain under dripping trees. He wants to holler it to every lit window, to every student in his or her numinous haze of thought. 'They *close!*'

He saw it with his own eyes: potassium channels that *closed*.

They did just the opposite of what everyone expected.

He assumed some sort of experimental error. He went back through Günter's contact sheets. He checked the amp and the connections. He wondered if he wasn't merely observing his own wishful thinking. He started again. He shook things up. He subjected the cells to change – changes of voltage, of ions, of temperature. Antony asked, morosely, for permission to leave early. He had an exam – Gross Anatomy – the next day. Didn't Antony understand? 'They're not simply open,' he announced over a new ten-pound cylinder of graph paper. 'They *open*ed.'

Antony's face was blank as an egg.

Günter suggested they call it a day.

But the channels opened. They were active. They opened *and*, more remarkably still, they *closed*.

Ella was right. He can't wait to tell her she was. The channels aren't merely passive conduits. They're not just machinery or component parts. They're alive and responsive. The evidence was there all along.

Somehow – he doesn't know how – she allowed him to see it.

Too many ions inside the cell – too much stress, exercise, anger, love, lust or despair – and they close. They stop all incoming electrical traffic. They preserve calm in the midst of too much life.

He can hardly believe it himself. The heart 'listens' to itself. It's a beautiful loop of feedback. Its parts listen to each other as surely as musicians do in an ensemble. No, forget the ensemble. The heart is an *orchestra*. It's the BBC Proms. It's more than the sum of its parts.

And what if the heart doesn't stop at the heart? What if the connections don't end?

Even he doesn't quite know what he means by this.

He will ask Ella. He will tell her of their meeting at the kissing gate.

Ella at eight.

He waits by the window until the lights go out over Tavistock Square and the trees melt into darkness.

He waits for three days. He retreats under the eider-down. He is absent from the slaughterhouse, the lab and the basement.

A fortnight passes. A month. Then it's new year.

When the second movement of the Piano Trio rises through the floorboards, he feels nothing. It has taken him months, but finally, he feels nothing.

As he comes round, the insult of the tube down his throat assures him he hasn't died.

The first thing he sees is his grandson by the foot of his bed, tapping away on his new mobile phone. 'Hi, Granddad,' Josh says, as if Denis has only been napping. He bounces to the side of the ICU bed, unfazed by the bleeping monitors and the tubes. 'Put your index finger here, Denis. I'll help you . . . No, like right *over* the camera lens. That's it. This phone has an Instant Heart Rate App. We'll see if you're working yet.'

'Cool,' Denis starts to say, but the irony is lost to the tube in his throat.

Josh's brow furrows. He studies his phone screen like a doctor on a medical soap. 'Sixty-two beats per minute at rest. Congratulations, Granddad. You're like . . . alive.' Josh squeezes his hand and grins.

Denis has never been so glad to see him.

On the other side of the bed, his wife touches his shoulder. Her face is tired. The fluorescence of the lights age her. She has lipstick on her front tooth and tears in her eyes as she bends to whisper, hoarsely, in his ear. 'You came back to me.'

The old words.

After a week, he'd given up hope. He realised he didn't even know where she lived, which student residence, which flat, which telephone exchange. He'd never thought to ask. Once he even tried waiting for her outside the Old Bailey, but the trial was over, someone said. Days before. Didn't he read the papers?

When she opened his door in January of '61, she stood on the threshold, an apparition. She simply waited, her shiny hair still flying away from her in the light of the bare bulb on the landing. He was standing at the window through which he'd given up looking. On the other side, the copper beech was bare with winter. In the room below, the Schubert recording was stuck on a scratch.

Her words, when they finally came, rose and fell in a rhythm he'd almost forgotten. 'Why don't you *know* that you're in love with me? What's wrong with you, Denis Noble?'

Cooking smells – boiled vegetables and mince – wafted into his room from the communal kitchen.

Downstairs, the cellist moved the needle on the record.

'You came back to me,' he said.

As his recuperation begins, he will realise, with not a little impatience, that he knows nothing at all about the whereabouts of love. He knows only where it isn't. It is not in the heart, or if it is, it is not only in the heart. The organ that first beat in the depths of Ethel in the upstairs room of Wilson & Jeffries is now consigned to the scrapheap of cardiovascular history. Yet in this moment, with a heart that is not strictly his, he loves Ella as powerfully as he did the night she reappeared in his room on Tavistock Square.

But if love is not confined to the heart, nor would it seem is memory confined to the brain. The notion tantalises him. Those aspects or qualities which make the human condition human – love, consciousness, memory, affinity – are, Denis feels more sure than ever, *distributed* throughout the body. The single part, as Ella once claimed so long ago, must contain the whole.

He hopes his new heart will let him live long enough to see the proof. He wishes he had a pencil.

In the meantime, as Denis adjusts to his new heart hour by hour, day by day, he will demonstrate, in Josh's steadfast company, an imperfect but unprecedented knowledge of the lyrics of Jay Z and OutKast. He will announce to Ella that he is keen to buy a BMX bike. He won't be sure himself whether he is joking or not.

He will develop an embarrassing appetite for doner kebabs, and he will not be deterred by the argument, put to him by Ella, his daughter and Josh, that he has never eaten a doner kebab.

He will surprise even himself when he hears himself tell Mr Bonham, during his evening rounds, that he favours Alton Towers over the Dordogne this year.

Sylvia Wears Pink in the Underworld

It's a cheek for me to say it, but this is no place for you.

'A cheek'. Not our native usage. I know. After all these years, I pick, I choose. English, North American. North American, English. I imagine you did the same. And wasn't it sweet to see Ted, in *Birthday Letters,* celebrating, *not* your 1956 Veronica Lake 'fringe', but your Veronica Lake 'bangs', or, if I'm being honest, your 'bang'. A fond concession to our vernacular – even if he got it wrong. More than once. Couldn't you just swat him with a dish towel and a newly-wed's grin. My *what?*

Your bang.

Oh, Ted!

I see you smooth your apron and its scattering of tiny red hearts. He winks at you over the *Observer,* and you turn away, knowing how grab-able your waist looks from behind. You concentrate on your Tomato Soup Cake recipe. Two cups sifted flour. One tablespoon baking powder . . . You long for the reliability of Campbell's condensed tomato soup. You feel wistful at the memory of those bright red-and-white cans which you skated on as a child across your mother's kitchen floor.

In the distance, near the entrance to the cemetery, three elderly women in dark woollen coats look my way – and yours – their jaws as square as paving slabs. (Don't ever let anyone tell you there aren't *some* advantages in not making it past the menopause.) Above them, above us all, in the strumpety June sunshine, St Thomas's dark tower rises like a reproachful finger.

There seems no denying it. You *were* a handful. It seems there were times when you could have worn out life itself, but the stony digit of that tower disapproves too much.

Of course. Thoughtless of me. The view from the Underworld *must* be limited; like the view round a pillar in a back row of the stalls. Only – yes – your 'pillar' is big, broad and everlasting.

Think back.

Through the dandelion spores of the centuries and across the buttercupped lane, the most ancient graves nestle closer to the church than yours, as no doubt you recall from Sunday afternoon strolls with Ted, and Christmas Day trudges through the snow and the mud with the in-laws.

How wrong you must have looked here.

When I arrived in 1987, I discarded every bright skirt and top I'd packed. I was afraid of blotting the streetscapes of England with too much colour. Like you, I learned how to be less vivid. I found Topshop, a houndstooth skirt and a dark, oversized cardigan.

Ahead of us, a mother and her two young daughters, both in pink Crocs, are running in a careless hopscotch across the slabs of the dead. I want to cheer at the twenty-first-century triumph of those Crocs, here of all places, but – yes – I understand. The living *are* thoughtless, running across graves, canoodling at kissing gates, making brass rubbings, and – you're quite right – being *overfamiliar*.

Today, a rock balances on top of your headstone. Beneath it lies a crushed daisy. Under the daisy are words in blue biro on a torn scrap.

I make Cakes too.
Life is a Dream.
Death is the reallity.

You wouldn't have bargained on this downturn in circumstances: on the ghetto of Deadland, the utter voicelessness, and now, to add insult to injury, misspelled poetic offerings from God knows whom. You couldn't have imagined it – not really, not you, not after *Mademoiselle* magazine, Cambridge camaraderie and vol-au-vents with the Eliots.

Let's change the subject.

Down the church path and through the gate, this bit of the village greets modernity with unexpectedly wide, perpendicular streets. Lawnmowers drone and dog walkers genuflect, their hands ritually sheathed in plastic. Somewhere a mobile incants 'The Birdie Song'. Wild roses blow. The foxgloves rise, their pink mouths electric with bees. In suburban-esque gardens, clumps of forget-me-nots insist as delicately, and as forgettably, as they do every year. (They are pale things compared with the wild alkanet that has colonised your grave.) Near the start of the footpath, ferns uncurl, tentative as new foetuses, while a man in long shorts and socks is, even here, on the blunt edge of a dark valley, washing and waxing his Ford.

If you watch carefully, you'll see the scenery of this village shake when the wind blows too hard. The symmetry of the newer streets is a hard-won make-believe.

At the village's heart, the soot-dark ginnels and archways still remember an emptiness – a wind-shot summit, the strange glow of moorland – while at the edge, the trees won't grow upright. They know the truth, as do the drystone walls that tremble at the lure of gravity. Down the sheer wall of woodland, among the wych elm and oak, an odd shoe, a glinting wine bottle and a baby's rusting pushchair are only the most recent sacrifices. The giddy swoop of the valley, the mesmerism of the river and the lush, leafy-green darkness can't help but draw everything down, down, down.

It must take a collective act of the villagers' will not to give in, not to be seduced, not to wobble too far in their stoical perch high on this hilltop.

This is not the place for you. You need sea level. You're a long way from the Cape Cod trance of Nauset's crashing rollers. Right now, there's no imagining you – *wishing* you – up to your elbows in rock pools, your hands rising with sand dollars, starfish and fiddler crabs. At night, you won't don your red bikini for a swim in the flashing phosphorescent surf. The sand dunes and their long grasses won't be disturbed by your body holding fast to his.

To your right, your neighbour is Horace Draper, the dearly loved husband of Emily, who lived his span of eighty-five years. To your left is Francis Joseph Carr, who left this world in November 1960, just days before Kennedy was elected to office. As Francis breathed his last, you squinted at a flickering black-and-white set in a shop window on Regent's Park Road, transfixed by the sight of the President-elect and Jackie standing on the brink of the decade outside their Hyannis Port home. You'd never say it, you'd only hope it, but weren't you and Ted almost as winsome in literary London? Your first collection was just out with Heinemann. The BBC was paying Ted well. Your kitchen calendar at Chalcot Square was marked by plans for appleseed cake, banana loaf and home-made waffles. In little over a week, you'd record 'Candles' and 'Leaving Early' for the *Poet's Voice*. You'd done the undo-able: you were the American sweater girl who'd become a British poet. England had let you moult your gung-ho, straight-A self.

On Regent's Park Road, you strain to read Kennedy's lips through the glass, to hear the New England burr of his words. Jackie smiles up at you, squinting into the Cape Cod sun. You can almost feel the sea-spangled light on your face. You can almost smell the salt marshes off the Nantucket Sound. JFK lifts Caroline into his arms. You jiggle Frieda in her pram and raise the hood against the drizzle. The parcel of pork loin is a reassuring weight in the shopping bag that dangles from your arm.

Did you know then? Did Ted? Already your marriage had failed.

Alkanet grows on disturbed ground. It can sting like nettles. Though classified as a weed, it is not so coarse that it lacks a Latin designation. *Pentaglottis* – 'five-tongued' – *sempervirens* – 'always alive'.

The only bouquet at your grave today is a spray of red-and-white carnations, but their blooms have withered in the bushy, two-foot-high shadow of the alkanet. Its tiny flowers have the dark plutonic brilliance of blue LED bulbs. Once upon a time, its huge taproot was cultivated by monks for cloth the colour of Christ's wounds, and, earlier still, by Egyptian priestesses to henna their hair. Red is of course your signature colour, the trademark hue of your tulips and poppies; of the bleeding cheeks, sliced thumbs and pulpy hearts you could not resist.

(Sssh. Lie low. Don't move. No rising up. The three Fates of Heptonstall have trained their eyes upon us.)

I don't see it at first amid the stalks of alkanet: a neat willow basket propped on your grave and packed with solid earth. Soil and mulch from someone's New England garden, or so says the smeared gift card.

I resolve not to look in the basket; not to intrude on your privacy and hers. Except I do. When the dark woollen backs of the Fates are turned, I hunker down and reach inside. And behold! It's as if the Welcome Wagon ladies have been.

First, a few silver coins – for the ferryman naturally. Will you need them now? I wonder. You're no longer that new soul waiting for the ferry, mistaking it for the 11 a.m. from Hyannis to Nantucket. I imagine you used to enjoy that journey simply for the to-and-fro of the ride itself. It would have offered you a rare release from *purpose*, from the need to *get* somewhere in life. Perhaps you like to ride the ferry, even now.

Next, a plastic ballpoint pen, red.

Drawing pencils and a pencil sharpener.

A chunk of pink rock. No, pink glass. Sea glass, if I'm not mistaken. Worn smooth.

A string of beads, white against the dark earth.

A string of black beads looped around the basket's handle.

A key ring with a pendant of tarnished silver. No key.

A three-inch female nude in red clay. She's big-breasted, big-bottomed.

Two red gummy children, sticky with the warmth of June.

An overturned red wine glass. Because you and Ted never *were* the types to reach for a plastic planchette. You doubted that Parker Brothers could point the way to the spirit world.

My childhood Ouija Board sat on a basement shelf beneath the Monopoly and Scrabble. I still remember the injunctions the kids down the street breathed into my ear. If the planchette falls from the board, a spirit will get loose. If you try to burn the board, it will scream. Never ask it when you're going to get rich or when you're going to die. Never, never use the planchette when you're alone.

I lift the glass from the basket. I dispense with formalities: the ring of paper letters, the 'yes' and the 'no', and a partner's fingertips on the base of the glass. Speed is of the utmost, for the Fates are coming my way, bearing garden spades and plastic floral features. Perhaps they are the sisters of Horace Draper, aged eighty-five. I, on the other hand, am disturbing a grave. Or at least a basket.

I hold the rim of the glass to my ear, as if I were listening for our crashing Atlantic three thousand miles away.

At first I hear nothing but the buzzing of the tinnitus I've had since dinner at a noisy Carluccio's the other week. The stalwart Fates trudge past, eyeballing me but saying nothing. Knitting needles and grey yarn poke from the pocket of the eldest. Overhead, swallows scissor the reams of sky, and something in the atmosphere opens.

Your voice comes, as crackly as an early BBC recording.

'*Love . . . life,*' you intone.

The first and last words of 'Ariel' zip and burn like supernovas through the stem of the glass.

What to say? 'May I ask where you are?'

'Oh . . . you know. On the river. The two of us.'

'The river.' So casual. So brave. I picture the smoking water of the Styx, the bitumen-light.

But no.

'We're gliding under an ornamental bridge with not a—' I lose your voice for a moment. 'We've commandeered a Swan Boat!'

I imagine oversized fibre-glass wings and a lurid plastic beak. Ted in a Swan Boat?

'It's been *years*,' you continue. 'Why, it's practically the Boston Public Garden.' If you try, you say, you can imagine your newly-wed apartment on Willow Street, as if it's just a walk away. Your white-and-gold Samsonite luggage is piled high in the swan's stern, and today you are wearing the eponymous Pink Wool Knitted Dress Ted tells us you were married in.

At my ear, the rim is as hot as an ancient fire cup. The base of the glass starts to vibrate against my palm. The strain of dimensions is too great. 'And Ted?' I call.

It's as if you're fiddling with an earpiece. 'Could you repeat the question?'

'Ted?'

'Yes,' you echo, '*Ted*. He's here too.'

'Is he enjoying the . . . the outing?' Somewhere to my left, the Fates are clattering away with their spade.

'That's – right,' you say. 'He's . . .'

'Could you—' A hairline crack is zigzagging up the bowl of the glass. 'Are you—'

'He's—'

'—happy?'

'—baiting a line. The fishing is good, we're told.'

'In the Styx?'

'Hold on . . . The man is telling me . . .'

'I'm sorry?'

'—we're nearly there.'

Through the splintering glass, your voice rises like a girl's and, somewhere up ahead, fish gleam and flash for you.

There are precious things

on the 4.38 out of Mile End.

In carriage three, Tanisha drops into a seat. Today, her mother arrived late to look after Obi, and now she is worried she will be late for her shift for the third time this month. Each afternoon, when Obi comes home from school, she looks at his new drawings or marvels over the words in English he has learned to spell. Then her mother comes – today bearing electric Christmas candles from the Pound Shop – and Tanisha sprints from her door to the Underground. Sometimes she wonders that so much of her life can pass below ground. Each day, she travels from her basement flat to the Central Line, from the Central Line to the Victoria Line and from the Victoria Line to the ladies' toilets beneath Victoria Station, where she is the evening attendant.

Last week, when her mother was laid low with flu, she had no choice but to take Obi with her. She cleaned, then closed a stall, and Obi sat inside, legs crossed on the toilet lid with his colouring book in his lap. But whenever she turned, he was out again, grinning over the Dyson Airblade, watching the flesh on his chubby hand ripple in the blast of air. The next day her supervisor informed her that a woman had complained about a boy of ten in the ladies' loos. Tanisha explained that Obi is only seven. She is on her final warning.

She opens her bag and takes out his letter to Father Christmas. It's written in tipsy purple letters, and he wants three things: a radio-control helicopter, a sledge and a Dyson Airblade. She told him that Father Christmas doesn't make air blades, but he shook his head earnestly and told her she was wrong. She cannot bring herself to say there is never snow for a sledge in Mile End, only dirty slush. Nor can she tell him that a radio-control helicopter needs a back garden.

In their language, Obi means 'heart'. She cannot be late today.

As the train leaves the station, carriage three jolts as if it wants to leap the rails, and the square of Obi's letter flutters to the floor, landing between the feet of the young man across from her. He's reading sheet music. Tanisha wonders whether she can pluck up the letter without disturbing him, but Edgar spots the bit of paper next to his oversized trainer and returns it with a smile.

At Bethnal Green, Edgar and Tanisha watch a nun board the train. For a moment it seems as if her brown habit will be caught in the closing doors, but she yanks it free just in time and meets Tanisha's eyes, smiling mischievously, like a white-haired child in her sixties.

It is standing room only. Edgar rises, shuffling his music, and offers Sister Kate his seat who thanks him, touching his shoulder lightly. Some part of the nun, Edgar cannot help but notice, is whistling in the key of D. He does not know that in the whorl of each of Sister Kate's ears sits a newly fitted hearing aid.

The harsh lighting makes bone and shadow of every face.

Sister Kate reaches up to adjust the tiny dial on each of her hearing aids, as her audiologist showed her, and she ceases to whistle. Each year she ventures just once out of the convent in Notting Hill to travel down the Central Line to the Bethnal Green clinic and back again. Each year she hears less and less, and curiously perhaps for a nun in a silent, cloistered order, she dreads the thought of being cut off from the song of the world.

She wakes each morning to the convent bell. Her room is next to the bakery, and as her eyes open, her heart remembers its rhythm in the automated thumps of the altar-bread press that resound through the party wall. She loves the soft shuffle of shoes as the women move towards morning prayer, and at teatime, the Prioress's voice rings out as delicately as a percussionist's triangle. Even the sound of Sister Martha taming the fruit trees in the garden with her electric hacksaw is somehow a delight to her ear.

There is so much to love.

A group of builders stands above her, joking – in Polish, she believes. She can smell the cool air of December coming off them. One – a husky man with bright apple cheeks – grins and bats his eyelashes at his friend, who, in reply, reaches towards the red lever of the passenger alarm.

Sister Kate thrills to their antics. Then she reaches into her carrier bag and takes out her knitting. The visitors' shop at the convent is selling hand-knit mobile phone covers, and the pattern is simple enough.

In the seats around her, many of her fellow travellers appear to be reading their phones. It is a concept she fails to understand.

She glances at the watch the Prioress has lent her. She must be back by vespers. The sweetness of those evening devotions is the closest she has come to joy, and she must be content with that. She has not felt a union with her god since the dream she had as a novice, age twenty, when she woke brimming with a love so unconditional, so full, her face streamed with tears. In those moments, there was no one and nothing of which she was not a part. But in her forty-four years of prayer and contemplation, that tidal wave of love has never picked her up again.

Two seats away, a woman holds a small dark-haired boy in her lap. He clutches a plastic toy. Sometimes, as now, Sister Kate tries to imagine the faces of the children she did not have.

The knitting needles tsssk and click between her fingers.

At Liverpool Street, the builders exit, the boy squirms in his mother's lap and shoppers with Christmas wrap poking from their bags settle into carriage three. Lionel is the last to board. He falls into a seat as the train lurches into motion.

To his left, a white guy about his own age grips the overhead rail; his other hand presses a sheaf of sheet music to his chest. Across the aisle, Lionel watches Tanisha, who is reading Obi's Father Christmas letter again. Next to her, a nun is knitting something blue. When she looks up, he looks away and shifts in his seat.

Lionel feels odd sitting across from a nun with a semen sample in his shirt pocket. But Bart's Hospital is just a seven-minute walk from St Paul's Station. He timed it last week. The sample mustn't be more than an hour old. He is on track to hand it in to the Fertility Unit fifteen minutes before its expiry. The sample has to be kept at body temperature. They gave him what looked like a test tube and told him to travel with it as close to his person as possible.

Lionel has taken the past few hours off from the garden centre. His mouth dried up when his boss asked why – after all, they still have 500 Christmas wreaths to shift. On break, he tried to distract himself with November's issue of *Flowers R Us*, flipping to a random article about the common poppy. 'Over seven years,' it said, 'a pair of poppies will produce 820,000 million million million descendants.'

Bloody show-off poppies.

He and Jacinta have been trying for three years.

The other night, they watched a documentary about human conception. It showed the epic journey of the sperm to the egg from the sperm's point of view. Inside Jacinta lay a vast and indomitable mountain range. If a sperm was a lone man, the territory was five miles deep, two miles wide and hostile. There was killer acid. There were ninja antibodies. The cervix, apparently, was every sperm's nightmare.

Jacinta turned to him on the settee, her eyes big and tearful at the miracle of creation.

Last month, she checked out fine.

Sometimes, in the small hours, Lionel dreams he's a tree. He is fine and strong until the wind blows and he topples, because he's only a trunk and not a tree after all. He has no roots, and the falling sensation – always horrible – jolts him from sleep.

He doesn't know why he felt he should wear a suit and tie to deliver his sample.

Now, in the steel hum of carriage three, Lionel cups his hand over the bulge of the tube in his shirt pocket, as if he's cradling a small head against his chest.

The train hurtles through a tunnel, and the boy in his mother's lap starts to whimper.

Clifton can't remember how long he has been riding the Central Line. It is the longest journey possible on the Underground. Forty-six miles from Epping Station to West Ruislip. He remembers that.

He rode this line every day of his working life, getting off at Leytonstone and walking the mile to the school. He'd always wanted to be a history prof, not a senior schoolteacher hauling boys apart every lunch hour. All his life, dates and facts have roosted effortlessly in his head.

But this afternoon, he walked into the lounge and saw a strange woman sitting in the armchair next to their Christmas tree. She was reading a book by the glow of the lights, and she smiled at him as he passed.

Alice, his wife, was stripping the bed in their room. 'Who is that woman in our house?' he asked. 'What is she doing here?' His heart struck at his ribs.

'Ssssh now,' she said, squeezing his hand. 'That's Diane, our *fourth*. Our *baby*.'

She reached for the snap propped up on his chest of drawers. Four children grinned back at him: three boys and a girl. On the reverse was a list of names. The final line read: 'Our Diane. She has been in America for some years now but visits.' The handwriting was his.

His eyes filled. 'My God, Alice. What is *wrong* with me that I don't even know my own daughter?'

She sat him down on the bare mattress. She said the consultant had assured them that, along with the episodes of confusion, he would still experience *good* periods of lucidity. She explained that he forgets even the diagnosis, and that every other day she has to remind him. She said that each time she does, they go through the heartbreak of it all over again.

He pressed his fists to his eyes. He needed fresh air – 'to clear his head,' he said – but in that moment, he knew his head would never be clear again.

He clutches a ticket for Zone 6, the snap of their children and a photo-booth picture of Alice. On the back, in tiny letters, he sees his own writing again: 'Weekend at seaside, 1968. Alice in Kiss-Me-Quick hat.'

Yes, quick, Alice, quick. He imagines the softness of her lips. His thumbprint smudges her face. The carriage lurches sharply around a corner, and even now there are precious things.

Edgar has found a seat once more. The nun spotted it first, and, remembering that he gave up his seat for her, she nodded at him to take it – quick, quick, said her smile. Now he turns another page of music and follows the thread of his melody with his finger. Will the choir pull it off today?

He loves Tallis's six-part score. He can already hear the soaring harmonies and that vast tenderness of sound. He's one of the nine soloists, and in the fifth verse, the intervals must be perfect. He tries to remember where syllables cluster intricately over a note; where the breath is divided into semibreves. He thought James, their conductor, pompous when he said it, but now he understands: the polyphonic antiphon is, literally, breathtaking.

Ahead, through the grubby window of the carriage door, he can just see the back of James's head in carriage two. At six feet four, he's hard to miss, and today, apparently, at the moment of truth, he'll don a bright red woolly hat. 'On that platform,' he announced to the group, 'I shall be your beacon!'

They groaned in unison.

His fellow choristers, Edgar reassures himself, are dotted through the other seven carriages.

He always feels naked in the first tremulous moments, with no organ for accompaniment; with just the power of one voice passing a line delicately to the next. Today, they will feel more naked than ever. No cathedral. No church. No stage. No formal wear. James is calling it the choir's 'gift of song'. Not that they can advertise it. The element of surprise will be everything. Edgar just hopes no one heckles or tries to shove him on to the rails for a laugh.

'Into the fray!' James had said, and Edgar's stomach had seized up.

He deepens his breathing and begins to shape the lyrics on his lips, one phrase at a time, unaware he's murmuring aloud: *Gaude gloriosa Dei Mater* . . . Rejoice, O glorious Mother of God . . .

He hears every syllable of song, every beat, every voice and breath. Nothing is excess. Nothing is stray. Just one more stop and—

★

Clifton presses Alice's photo-booth picture to his chest.

Lionel shelters the sample in his shirt pocket.

Sister Kate looks up from her knitting and almost weeps at the sound of Edgar's gentle murmurings. (*Gaude gloriosa Dei Mater* . . . Rejoice)

In Tanisha's bag, Obi's letter to Father Christmas is safely stowed. When the little boy in the woman's lap squirms again and drops his toy, a plastic dinosaur, Tanisha bends quickly to retrieve it, jiggling his foot as she passes it to him.

The boy's mother turns, her face hard. 'Who said you could touch my son?'

'I'm sorry,' says Tanisha. 'I only—' She cannot get her English out quickly enough. She cannot say that, in Nigeria, children and old people are meant to be loved by everyone.

Edgar's eyes close. *Gaude Virgo Maria, cui angelicae turmae dulces in caelis resonant laudes* . . . Rejoice, O Virgin Mary, to whom the hosts of angels in heaven sweetly sing praises . . .

The mother's elbow nudges Tanisha in the ribs. 'Listen to yourself. You can't even speak English. What are you doing in this country?'

'I work,' says Tanisha. 'I do not take anything.'

'*I* used to work till' – She looks down the carriage and raises her voice – 'till you lot come over.'

'No British want my job,' says Tanisha.

'Pull the other one.'

'Excuse me?'

Edgar's eyes snap open and he glares at the mother. 'Ignore her. She doesn't deserve a reply.'

Across the aisle, Lionel leans forward in his seat, still cradling the sample. 'Get this straight, yeah? I'm

British, lady. Most of the people on this train is British.'

'And I'm Nelson Mandela!'

Clifton starts to rock in his seat, hands pressed to his ears. Who is this woman? And where *is* Alice?

Edgar cannot lose the words. *Gaude flos florum speciosissima* ... Rejoice, most beautiful flower of flowers ...

Clifton fumbles for his mobile phone. 'Alice, Alice? Where am I? For Lord's sake, tell me where I *am* ...' He forgets that the Central Line runs deep, and there is no signal.

fessi cura ... succour of the weary ...

Sister Kate bows her head, finds a still, innermost place and prays as the woman begins to rant.

'I will ask you politely, yeah?' says Lionel. 'Would you please leave this train?'

'Me? It's you lot who need to leave!' She eyeballs Lionel, Tanisha and Clifton.

Voices. Such noise, such terrifying noise. Clifton stumbles to his feet. He looks around the carriage, wild-eyed. Everyone is a stranger. 'Stop!' he cries out, 'please stop!' as the train pulls into St Paul's, and Edgar, music in hand, leaps from the train to the platform, where James the conductor lifts his arm, and the voice of the first soloist rises.

The notes soar, like Lionel's hope as he sprints away, palm pressed to his pocket; like the wave of love that lifts Sister Kate at last, there in the ugly light of carriage three, where Tanisha takes Clifton tenderly by the hand, as the voices swell and the harmonies surge, rising above the astonished crowd.

Oscillate Wildly

Many years after his great-uncle laid the solid round of it in his hand, he would think of the carving. In the stillness of near death, as the nurse pressed the sponge to his lips, he'd see in his mind's eye the creamy white stone gleaming on his desk. His fingertips would remember the rough edge where the vandal's hammer struck. He'd spare a thought for the poor, notorious penis that was severed with the blow and rested now, inert and foreshortened, on its cushion of stone testicles. Were he able to move his mouth, he would have smiled a final time at its comic vulnerability, naked on top of a pile of utility bills – his Great-uncle Gaston's erstwhile paperweight and, for a brief while longer, his.

In these moments, details took on a radiant clarity. They did so in spite of the injections of diamorphine – sweet, merciful heroin – that his brain now required to forget the tumour pain and to bypass the sensation that something was tearing into his gut.

How many days had passed like this? Three? Four? Through the floorboards, he could sometimes hear his ex-wife Shelley's muffled directives to their daughters. Often he woke to the sound of the nurse stirring sugar at the bottom of her coffee mug, or to the bass line of his neighbours' music reverberating through the party wall. More rarely, he heard the tight, compressed breathing of Eoin, his brother, as he turned the pages of the *Independent* beside his bed. At night, he listened to his lover, Abby, turn in her broken sleep on a rug on the floor across the room. Other sounds were initially harder to identify: the slow shuffle of his elder daughter's grief on the stairs; the angry jingling of his younger daughter's bracelets as she moved in and out of his room. Twice an hour, unmistakeably, the trains hurtled past the nearby crossing, as loud as avenging angels at the dead end of his street. He was fifty-two.

He had expected a heart attack. His doctor had explained that tumours need blood; that, in time, there wouldn't be blood enough for him and them both. He had imagined himself reading at his desk as the ghostly boot-blow was dealt to his chest, and Abby or one of the girls finding him, upright, in his black jeans and green pullover, resigned, gone, but okay. He hadn't expected to wake, without actually waking, to cold, soaked sheets below him; to the sensation of a catheter being threaded through him. He wouldn't have believed that he, he who'd always been so able to turn a phrase, would some day communicate his thoughts in a code of stuttering eyebrows and eyelids.

More than anything, he would never have dreamed that his body was capable of such stillness.

Now, the brightness of the room seeped through his eyelids. Flies were buzzing against the skylight's pane when he felt Abby's hands on his feet, rubbing the soles.

Downstairs, Katie – or was it Sonia? – thumped across the floor to answer the phone. Beside his bed, a newspaper rattled. His brother had entered the room.

Abby said, 'I'll just go for a Nescafé, Liam. I won't be long. Eoin's here with you now.' Then, as if taking her cue, Eoin's hand, cold with nerves, found his beneath the sheet, and Liam felt again the vibrations of his life.

He'd last held his brother's hand in 1957 as they queued to see *Calamity Jane* at the Imperial Cinema. Calamity had arrived in Belfast in '54, but she didn't make it to Newry until three years later. Liam was six years old; Eoin, ten, and already grave; grave for their father's sake, who didn't want his sons picking up the habits to which, he feared, they were, by birth, predisposed. Drink. Wildness. Music. Fast talk. Shallow charm. Hadn't his own brothers been prone to the worst excesses? Wasn't the border only a stone's throw? Weren't his own people, the native Irish, prone to trouble?

Yes. There they are, he and his brother. In the queue for the Saturday morning show, Liam begs his brother for an ice cream soda but Eoin only frowns, shakes his head and squeezes the half crown in his thin, hot hand.

Soon enough, Liam forgets all about Eoin's locked fist. He forgets about ice cream sodas. All he wants now is to be Wild Bill Hickok throwing Calamity Jane on to the horse-drawn cart and yee-hawing her out of Deadwood. He wants to be a squawling Indian brave, running in her wake. At the very end, when Calamity Jane swaps her buckskin and boots for a wedding dress, he wants to be the gun hidden in the bustle next to her backside.

Calamity Jane is Liam's first love, and all the way home, he swings on Eoin's arm, begging him to turn back for the afternoon show. 'Just once more, Eoin. Please, Eoin. Come on. Let's just see that fil-im again.

It was something, wasn't it? Didn't you think it was something? They won't even be home till suppertime. There's money enough. Let's just, why don't we, we've still time, and you could have my next week's allowance and my Atlas bodybuilder's book. Come on, Eoin. Eoin? Please, Eoin. Come on, please now, be a legend.' He swings madly on Eoin's arm.

Older now and bigger. At the strange cemetery a wind is blowing. The trees are bending and scraping like a rich man's servants; the pansies are flouncing, and Liam's running into the wind, his legs like pistons, his cheeks flattened and red.

His mam and his Great-uncle Gaston have slowed on the uphill walk. '*Attends! Attends!*' his mother calls, a ribbon of a voice in the wind. It is the first time she has spoken to Liam in her native French. He doesn't like it.

He runs past flower pots with rotting stems; past sad-faced stone ladies with their gowns sliding off their titties; past funny street signs at the junctions of the paths, as if this is actually a town of the dead; past graves that aren't graves but fancy stone houses with only one room because, he supposes, the needs of the dead are few. (*Why are cemeteries surrounded by fences? Because everyone's dying to get in. Ba-dum!* Tommy Murphy told him that one.)

He decides it is better to die in Ireland than in Paris because in Ireland the outdoors looks like the outdoors and gravestones are mossy and chipped, and the letters wear down with the wind and the rain so everyone gets forgotten in time, and life flies on.

But he won't tell his mother's uncle as much because Great-uncle Gaston is soon for the grave himself; he's the last of a generation, his mam explained, and that's why she's come and brought Liam for company, because he will make her old uncle laugh. It doesn't need to be said: neither Eoin nor their da would ever be able to make an old French uncle laugh. 'Oncle Gaston is big in his 'eart,' she says. ''E made me laugh when I was a little girl. This is where you get it.' It seems odd to Liam. An old uncle who likes to laugh who has worked all these years as a cemetery keeper.

When they are at home in Newry, Liam never thinks of his mam as French. In Newry, she's just 'foreign', and for Liam she's just his mam with her sing-song voice and her full lips that push out more than everyone else's when she speaks. He knows Jimmy Quinn from school fancies her when he serves her at the butcher's on Saturdays, and Liam could flatten him for it.

She arrived by accident in 1946 when the bus she was travelling on with her elderly boss, a respected French chocolatier, broke down in Newry. They were on their way from Dublin to Belfast where she was meant to take notes on chocolate distribution at J. Lyons and Co. When his da spotted her, smoking elegantly under the bus shelter on Canal Street, he drew breath at the sight of her legs crossed at the ankles and the red silk scarf tied at her neck. He was twenty-three and already bored by Irish girls and their eagerness to marry. When he heard her speak – to ask about lodgings for the night – he was beside himself with emotion for the first and last time in his life.

Liam knows the story. His father let it slip last year on St Stephen's Day after his annual glass of port. But the truth of the matter occurs to Liam only now as he runs towards the cemetery's far side: that he, Liam

O'Donnell, came into the world because of a bus's broken water-pump. It makes him laugh so hard he has to gasp for air as he runs. Wait till he tells Eoin that he's also on this earth because of a broken water-pump. Eoin won't like it. Not one bit.

He's grinning at the thought when he comes up short at the sight of the angel.

It's not a pretty angel this time with soulful eyes and a slippery dress. No. It's a big fucker with broad square wings rising from its back. And the face is ungodly, as Father Hurley might say. In fact, the angel looks too disdainful to bother with the likes of either Father Hurley or Liam. It looks in a mood, like Mr O'Flaherty the history master when he turns away from the boys, disgusted by their ignorance.

But the wings mesmerise Liam. They're powerful things that rise above his head, with long feathers carved into the stone, feathers that are longer even than those on an Indian brave's headdress.

He steps closer and, bending, peers at the naked angel's undercarriage, as a farmer might a bull's, because the angel isn't upright like a man. It has flanks, not a torso, and – he has to look twice – a broken stump of a penis without balls. Another faulty water-pump.

He turns at the sound of voices. His mother and her uncle have caught him up at last. Liam backs away from the stumpy remains, not knowing where to put his offending hand, but Uncle Gaston booms with laughter and crooks an arthritic finger. '*Viens*,' he rumbles.

They return to the keeper's house, a house which Liam is relieved to discover has three good-sized rooms, not the single room the dead seem to favour in Paris.

It is good to know that Great-uncle Gaston *is* indeed alive, even though his skin is almost see-through.

After all the sunshine outside, Liam has to blink himself back into the world. When he does, he finds his great-uncle pointing to a dusty metal desktop beneath the single window. And there they are, on top of a pile of papers. Oscar Wilde's angel's bits.

His uncle lifts the fragment of stone from the desk and lowers it into Liam's hand, wheezing with laughter.

'Heavy,' Liam says.

'*Mais oui!*' the old man declares.

Years later Liam will read about it: the public outrage at the monument, the tarpaulin, then the infamous blow of the hammer. But unknown to the official histories, the following morning the dutiful keeper collected the fallen fragment, wrapped it in a piece of chamois leather and returned to the keeper's house where he deposited it, sheepishly, upon his desk.

There it would remain. At the end of his tenure, he would bequeath the bollocks to the next keeper, who would in turn bequeath them to the next and so on, up and down the decades, until the day the *commune* took over from the *arrondissement* and deemed there would be no more permanent keepers. Uncle Gaston in his blue serge uniform was the last of a line, and in more ways than one. He and his wife had never had children.

The Newry postman could have had no idea of the contraband he delivered. The beloved bollocks arrived one summer's morning in a bundle of newspaper and a box marked 'M Liam O'Donnell'.

Liam's father and brother frowned at the sight but his mother reached up, put her arms around her son who was a head taller than she was and whispered in his ear that he should be proud. This was Art. History. Tradition. The sculptor wanted to show *life*, didn't he?

Just months later, on a November's day that never grew light, Liam would return home after school, late from dawdling in the record shop with Patrick Dunn, to find his mother dead. He can still feel the strange sensation of his legs giving way; can see her, pale against the feather bolster with the eiderdown riding up over her yellow-soled feet; can see his father at the mean window, upright in his dark tie and jacket, his face pinched.

'Another stroke,' Dr Kearney murmured. He bowed his big boiled-egg of a head. 'I'm very sorry.' He had a soft voice for so big a man. 'She was a wonderful woman, and too young.'

Liam's father nodded, bitterness seeping from him. 'I used to tell her . . . I used to tell her she needed to quit the gaspers, didn't I, Liam? Jesus, Mary and Joseph, I used to tell her.' He looked warily across the room to his younger son. 'Now don't be chivvying me with that black face of yours, not while your brother is already on his way to the rectory, making himself useful.'

Years away from Newry, in his attic room, on his own deathbed – a bed that obliges the visiting nurses to bend lower than their union permits – Liam hears once more his uncle's rumbling, laughing voice somewhere in the space between the bed and the eaves. As Abby lays her hand, cool and light, on his forehead, he hears his mother call again, '*Attends! Attends!*'

Because he's climbing into the van with the others. He should have scarpered when he had the chance, but it's too late now, and he's trembling like a fly on flypaper because the one in the black balaclava has already shown them the handgun beneath his donkey jacket. Liam has no idea where they're going. There are no windows in the van. All he can see is Neil in the seat across from him, worrying a stick of gum in its silver foil like it's a flaming rosary, and he has to shout over the roar of the engine, 'Neil, will you sit quiet, for Christ's sake!' But the one in the green ski mask stands up and punches him in the eye for speaking, and he's sure it's Jimmy Quinn who used to fancy his mam.

When they tumble out, there are only trees, tyre tracks and a few empty food tins by a fire pit. Their captors line them up against the van, heads down, hands where they can see them, legs spread – Seamus O'Shea, Tommy Murphy, Patrick Dunn, Neil Flynn and himself – in other words, all the Newry boys who are aiming for university – and Liam wants anything but this. This waiting. This limbo of dread.

All because Pat Dunn mouthed off in the pub last week over in Warrenpoint. He dubbed the Provos – Jimmy Quinn's gang – the goddamned mafia of Newry and now, now hours pass with the lot of them spread-eagled against the van, and the warning still ringing in their ears: 'The first one of yous that turns round is the first one to get it.'

Liam's hands are splayed against the dirty side, and he doesn't dare turn his face to catch the eye of Tommy who's beside him. He doesn't dare do anything but train his ears on the darkness, listening for any sign. He hasn't heard so much as a twig crack since before nightfall. Maybe his father was right about the Irish and trouble – because that's what they're calling it on the telly every night – The Troubles – and he's never been in such trouble in all his eighteen years.

By dawn, Seamus O'Shea is so sick and crazy with sleeplessness that he forgets *not* to look over his shoulder when the wood pigeons wake and flap in the trees. And, 'Thank Christ,' he says. 'They've fucked off. It was a goddamn wind-up.' But no one's laughing. Neil is throwing up into some bushes. Tommy is crying because he shat himself. Seamus and Pat start to row about Pat shooting off his mouth in that pub. Liam lies down on the ground and stares, with the eye that isn't swollen shut, at a sky he thought he'd never see again. There's a sliver of a moon so sharp you could cut your wrists on it.

A warning. Get out of town.

So he's on the ferry chucking up over the side and dodging Father Hurley who's going to visit his sister in Kilburn; he's old now but Liam can't forget how he used to try to get him to talk dirty in the confessional, so he lets Father Hurley smell the stink of vomit on his coat and he doesn't see him again.

Then it's 'No blacks, no dogs, no Irish' in every lodging-house window, and he's busking at Piccadilly, singing because that's what the English think the Irish should do at street corners, and he's got no address for Eoin who's God-knows-where in London, so things go from bad to worse till he starts pushing dope, which is how he meets Shelley. It's not love at first sight there in the subway below Piccadilly but he doesn't want romance – he just wants shelter, shelter – and Shelley is his harbour, all safe and mothering, and earning a wage too in an office somewhere. They're okay – she's not Calamity Jane and he's not Wild Bill – but it's okay, he makes her laugh and they marry because Shelley can't get into the Civil Service if they don't. The new flat isn't much and he can't afford to finish his A levels, but pushing is still better than busking, and soon enough he gets a real job, putting up sheds in the big gardens of rich Londoners so, for a while at least, at last, he and Shelley rest easy.

Only the carpet is sour, why does the carpet smell sour, did he knock over his beer? But he can't stop to think because they're on the floor, Shelley all soft and warm beneath him, and they're making a baby – 'Get drunk for a girl,' they used to say in Newry – but for all his humping, he can't come and Shelley says she's getting sore with him going at it. It's been nearly half an hour, and can't they turn the telly off? It's nearly over, he says, trying hard not to laugh at Frank and Betty Spencer who are in a hotel room for their second honeymoon. When Frank lowers Betty on to the bed, the bed collapses and Betty's shapely bottom bobs up, which is when Liam gives way at last, the tendons in his legs trembling like slingshots. Shelley lifts her legs into the air and stays like that, staring at the ceiling, all dreamy like, while Liam watches the end of the show. Then nine months later, Katie is born, and Liam falls in love all over again as he and Shelley fall out of love, if love – married love – it ever was.

By the time they decide that Katie needs a brother or a sister, Liam has been sleeping on the settee for nearly two years. At least he gets the work for his A levels done – better late than never – and after that, his degree. It's amazing how two people can share a home by stepping around one another. It's also uncanny how other women seem to know when you're not sleeping with your wife and put temptation in your way. Liam can only be grateful. And there's the garden centre van too, his home away from home, with his *Hamlet* exam quotations Sellotaped to the dashboard. But when Shelley tells him the calendar says go, all systems alert, he smiles cooperatively, and slips into his old room and in and out of her again, so that by the time he returns to the settee – his sperm more fervent than he – Sonia, his beautiful girl, is conceived.

Outside his attic room, the trains at the level crossing are getting louder and louder. Twice an hour they tear past, as if, at any moment, they'll explode into the room and bear him away. The four walls shudder, and he wonders blearily if death is as lonely a thing as those days long ago, after the split, when he ached for his baby girls. He worries for a moment about how the undertaker will get his body down from the attic – the staircase is narrow, steep and bending – it's a black comedy in the making – and he'd be the first to laugh if he weren't in a goddamn coma – *ha-ha* – and there weren't already tears slipping down his cheek. *Ba-dum!* 'Liam,' Abby lulls, 'sssh now. Ssh, sweetheart. I'm here. You're not alone.' He doesn't know whether to blink once for Yes, as in *Yes, I hear you, I understand* – or for, *Yes, I* am *alone, I'm alone in here and frightened.*

Abby. It's the college picnic and already he loves her but she's married and it isn't right, it isn't right, he knows full well, but it's midsummer and the grass in the clearing is long. It waves him on as he pulls off his shoes and socks, and runs madly forward into the handspring, his arms, back and legs moving into line . . . Then he lifts his left leg, extends his knee, plants his hands as far as he dares from his final step and kicks his right leg up, his body a perfect vertical, his abs tight as the blood rushes to his head. He pushes his arms back, arches his ribs, then springs forward to land, miraculously, on the balls of his feet.

It's thirty years since he captained the gymnastics squad in Newry, and he's lucky he didn't snap his spine. But she turned to watch.

Abby was born on the November day, the very day, they buried his mother. He was fifteen, lost and winded at the graveside in the hour she came keening into the world – and somehow that makes her dear to him. She's not fooled by his charm or his black Irish eyelashes like other women, but still, she laughs easily, and her words run deep within him. He wants to tell her she should, she really should, but she doesn't recoil from the bite of him when he goes mad on the booze and the shame of what he hasn't become. She doesn't turn and run from the rabid thing that curls in his gut and is turning, little by little, into the tumour they will cut from him years too late.

'Liam, listen,' she says, her head next to his now. Pillow talk. He dreams of her breast in his mouth. 'Can you hear it? The music. Next door's.' It's an instrumental, faint through the wall. He can't quite get it, though he was once an encyclopedia of song. It's a loop of sound: cool, restless, spooky. Then, against the odds, out of nowhere, it rises, a crescendo of something that sounds like joy.

'Oscillate Wildly'. The Smiths. And Abby's breath warm on his cheek.

Only there are footsteps now, heavy on the stairs – she's lifting her head off the pillow and Liam can't hear the music any more because Eoin is speaking from the foot of the bed. His brother, his long estranged brother, his sombre sibling, is saying, 'Abby, leave him. The girls should be at their father's side.' But Katie and Sonia are fine where they are, in the corner of his room, sifting old photos, content, near him but not so near that they're frightened by the sight of his wasted body beneath the sheets.

He can feel the strain of Abby's hand on his. She is afraid of Eoin, of his deadly earnestness. She is afraid to argue, to disturb the calm of the room, and Eoin is speaking to her like she is a servant of the house. *How dare you?* Liam wants to shout but his lungs can't find air and his lips won't move. Then her hand is leaving his, her voice is fading, he can hear her steps receding on the stairs – *Jesus, no – no, Abby—*

And he's on his feet, running – somehow – he has no idea how he's managed it – down the stairs – he's breathless behind her – why doesn't she turn? Every muscle in his legs is driving him forward as—

Great-uncle Gaston's cemetery flies past: the women in the slippery dresses, the houses of the dead and his mother too, a red scarf tied at her neck. The stone bollocks are heavy in his hand but he feels as if he could run for ever – *Abby!* – or he does until he finds himself face to face with Oscar Wilde's angel.

His uncle is at the grave already. The old man nods. Liam knows what he has to do. He unwraps their paperweight from the piece of chamois leather. He moves to the angel's side. Then he bends and slides the bollocks and their stump of a penis back into place.

The angel's flanks shudder to life. Its feathers ripple. Liam backs away and sees the impassive eyes blink, the mouth tense. He watches, dazed, as the monumental wings quiver, then beat the air, loud as a windmill's sails. He turns his face to an unsettled sky and stares as the angel heaves itself into flight.

In those moments, in that dizzying commotion of shadows, air and light, Liam feels again the wild oscillations of his life: the swinging, the running, the trembling, the chucking-up, the busking, the pushing and the humping; his sperm swimming, his babies babbling, Hamlet soliloquising, his body handspringing, his eyelids blinking, the joy rising and those wings spreading, defiant and tremendous, as the train at the crossing tears past.

Dreaming Diana: Twelve Frames

I

I can admit it now.

In 1981, I had the Lady Di. I went to Wendy's Hair Salon on the Bedford Highway and asked for the Lady Di because I didn't know the name of any other haircut, except the Farrah Fawcett, and I didn't have the nerve to ask for those feathery wings that were emblematic of Farrah's pin-up glory.

Wendy cut my hair herself, and didn't laugh when I asked for the Lady Di, but even she, sucking hard on her cigarette, couldn't work that magic. On my lap lay a picture of Diana at the London nursery where she worked. She had a child on each hip, and the sun was streaming through her cotton skirt. She looked melancholy. She wouldn't smile for the photographer; I liked her for that. The article said the silhouette of her legs through her skirt was a sensation. I didn't understand. Everyone had legs.

At Wendy's Hair Salon, locks of dark hair fell across my knees to the floor. I emerged from the salon looking like a boy. A pageboy. A pageboy without long legs.

Still, that summer, aged sixteen, three years younger than Diana, nothing was impossible. I'd fallen in love with Stephen Murray. He was tall. He had a dry wit. He spelled his name with a 'ph' instead of a 'v'. It made him complicated.

On midsummer's eve, the final dance of the school year was held, not in the gym, but at the Harbour Boat Club in the city. Gone was the smell of rubber crash-mats and adolescent sweat; gone, the generalised threat of gym ropes and foul lines. Instead we stepped on to a sunken dance floor with parquet tiles. We bloomed against crêpe-paper streamers and bright Chinese lanterns. Outside, on the long, low veranda, boys threat-ened to let the girls in their arms drop into the tide below while, above us all, the Northern Lights shook the night sky.

I can't remember the song. I only remember that as Stephen Murray and I started to dance, he turned me on my heels and my pale yellow skirt took life, floating wide as a water lily on the air.

We walked through the night together. He took my hand in his. We tried to remember what caused the Northern Lights and couldn't. We skimmed stones across the ebbing waves. Friends discovered us on the shore and, within moments, everyone was peeling off shoes and socks, and wading into the surf. Mighty splashes of water fanned high into the night. We girls screamed and ran laughing from the shallows up the beach, cold water dripping down our breastbones, arms and legs, marking our dresses and skirts. But when I looked back over my shoulder to find Stephen in the night, he was nowhere. I walked down the beach and called his name. Finally, I gathered up my shoes and spotted him striding up the hill towards the Club, where the paper-lantern light trembled in the dark.

Back inside no one knew where he was. I thought, I'll find him on Monday in English class. Or I'll pretend to discover him in the library. *Ah! You're working in here too?* He'll forgive my joining in with the others on the shore, and he'll smile at me across the examinations hall.

Moments before the last dance, Stephen reappeared. I spotted the dim outline of him beyond the entrance, and I stood from the table where I'd been seated, marooned with friends. Behind my back, my hands were clasped, and my pulse raced in my thumb. As he crossed the threshold, I couldn't help myself; I walked towards him. His eyes were adjusting to the light. Could he see me?

Then, as he approached the dance floor, something extraordinary happened. A girl materialised at his side: a girl I had never seen, a girl no one had ever seen, a girl from out of town who seemed in that moment more conjured than real. The magic of the night forked. I watched him introduce her to his friends. She was tall, elegant. 'This is Diana,' I heard him say.

In that moment I envied her her name, her height and her mystery, but even more than these things, I envied her her hair. She had a perfect Lady Di, a cloud of gold dipping over one eye.

Like everyone that summer, I watched the Royal Wedding and cried.

2

Two years later, I couldn't explain to myself why I was waiting to see Diana. The lobby of the Hotel Nova Scotian was empty. A British photographer was asleep on his feet against a pillar. My sister Ellen wanted to go home. She was too blasé for royalty. Privately, I wished I was as well. I rooted in my bag and pulled out the Kodak camera our parents had given me for graduating so successfully that year.

Bear in mind I was too proud to pin any pop poster to my bedroom wall. Instead I'd Blu-tacked into place a Bruegel print of dancing peasants. I had standards. Yet here I was, following the crowd. Or rather, I would have been following the crowd had we not arrived two-and-a-half hours before any crowd.

Ellen looked at my camera and rolled her eyes. 'Tell me you're *not* going to take pictures.'

I played with the Instamatic shutter. I stared at the ceiling of the lobby, avoiding her stare, for I could already imagine Diana's foot stepping on to the red carpet the two bellboys were unfurling before us. She would move. Smile. Extend her hand. Perhaps she would say a few words in passing. All in three dimensions.

We rationed the Smarties Ellen had in her school bag. We found two pens and played tic-tac-toe on her bare, restless legs. For a long time, we watched the British photographer not wake up.

Time passed reluctantly. Bystanders turned into a crowd, and the crowd into a throng. We held our ground. The lobby grew hot, airless. The floral top I'd made in Home Economics that year was sticking to my armpits, and my camera was sweating like old money in my hands.

When the moment was at last upon us, I hesitated. Prime Minister Trudeau walked through the door in his white dinner jacket and black bow-tie.

Diana was just moments behind. Charles was – I was relieved to see – already working the other side of the red carpet.

Was it better, I asked myself, to watch her 'live' – perhaps to shake her hand – or to get a picture? A picture of a picture coming to life.

She was wearing a pale-yellow chiffon ball gown and a tiara. Her hair was longer than I'd seen in any of the photos, and she was very slim. Her face was lowered in her trademark way, but now and again as she walked, she peered out from beneath her golden bangs.

How strange for her, I thought. *She can only be thinking, Where am I? Why did I never do a geography O level?* She would have looked fragile were it not for the strength of that wide, generous smile.

She was shaking hands, smiling, saying hello, asking the occasional question. I remember the novelty of hearing her speak as I watched her through my camera's viewfinder. She stopped and said a few words to the hotel receptionist next to Ellen. I raised my camera. I felt self-conscious – rude – as I pointed it at her. I faltered, lowered my arm. Then I took the picture.

Or four, to be precise.

Later, everyone marvelled that I'd been so close, that I'd managed to get such good shots. 'She looks beautiful,' they said.

'She's more so in real life,' I heard myself say.

I sounded absurd to myself. What did it actually matter to any of us what she looked like?

They waited for a spree of adjectives, for my youthful eyewitness account, but I didn't have the words. Not because I'd had any pang of conscience, but because I couldn't describe the surprising *light* of her. It wasn't flashbulbs. Or the glamour of a blonde. Or the radiance of a new bride. It wasn't any of those things.

Afterwards, I stuck the snaps in a new album. I took care to avoid ripples as I pressed them under the transparent sheet. But you can't get a picture of a picture coming to life. Reality collapses. It's simply another picture.

3

Faster now. Time is rushing on.

It's July '97. My marriage to Jon is just six years old. To all outward appearances, we are a lovely young couple, perfectly suited. Everyone tells us so. Yet there's a mystery I can't unravel; a problem that hovers just out of reach, indecipherable as Jon's face when I ask him what the matter is.

We are not, I know, like other couples in their twenties. I ask my young, handsome husband why he loves me and does not love me. But each time I do, his words reassure me, though his eyes – all strain and kindness – do not, and the mystery of our marriage refuses to leave our little whitewashed cottage with the vegetable patch in the back garden and our bikes at the door. It will declare squatter's rights. On weekends, it will read the Sunday papers alongside us and huff its stale breath across our table. It will lie between us at night, a strange third life in our big pine bed.

Days before our wedding, Jon's brother asked him if he was sure he was doing the right thing. When Jon told me of the question – giving it sudden weight in the world with its repetition – my heart stammered. I could only say, 'Really? Why would he ask that?'

Our date was set. At the altar, Jon's eyes filled as he looked into mine and said his vows. Later, he clasped me to him as the camera flashes went off in the nave. 'Look,' my smile my told my husband's brother. 'How wrong you were.'

But something was not right. The mystery hovered even there in our country church as the bells pealed. Jon's right arm did not hold mine fast as we walked down the aisle; it did not bend to link with mine or to receive my hand as my father's had. That night, in a wide four-poster, he told me we were both tired after the full day. Given our year of cohabitation, it was fine for us simply to sleep.

His mother *adored* her two sons. She declared often and with ease that she was delighted she had never had girls; that girls were trouble; that her boys, husband and father were the joy of her life.

When she kissed each adult son, and especially her firstborn, the duration of her kisses surprised me. When she was tired, she would rest her body against Jon's chest, lay her head on his shoulder, smile dreamily and close her eyes. He neither yielded to her nor resisted, but tolerated her need with love, and with an inborn understanding of human frailty.

Only years later did I learn that Jon had discussed his heart's confusion with his mother. She had counselled him, explaining gently and lovingly that the best thing one could do in life was to marry one's best friend. Not to choose a lover who might in time become a best friend, but rather to marry a girl who would, from the outset, be his reliable friend. Nothing mattered more. Perhaps even she did not fully realise that a half-marriage for her son was the most she could bear. In the months leading up to our wedding, she was often mysteriously unwell.

It would be several years before I would learn that my marriage had been arranged around me; before I would understand that, although I had married for love, I was not beloved.

Five years of friendship passed. The third thing in our bed grew restive. It got bigger, heavier. Jon grew thin. He could hardly eat, no matter how busily I cooked and baked; no matter how wifely I became.

Then, during a trip to Paris in which we tried to divert ourselves from our unhappiness, I found myself standing at a news kiosk and staring at front-page tabloid snaps of Diana in profile. She was walking barefoot on a sandy beach in the Med, holidaying with her boys and her new 'companion', Dodi Fayed. Here she was, emerging from the broken spell of the wedding 750 million had witnessed. Even Diana, it seemed, had never truly been wanted.

In the photos, she was wearing a one-piece swimsuit, an animal print. Her head was down. She was refusing to look the way of the offshore boats. Her arms were folded over her front.

Perhaps her posture was, at that moment, poor. Perhaps she had a tummy that day.

'DIANA ENCEINTE?' the tabloids speculated.

She was a vessel for us to fill.

4

Slide the transparent strip through your fingers. Hold it by the edges only, at the sprocket holes. Avoid fingerprints. (My own are already all over them.) Now lift it to the lamplight.

Frame 4. That's the one.

Grainy, yes.

They say, you wouldn't have known to look at her; her face was unchanged except for the bruising under one eye.

At the private mortuary in Fulham, the post-mortem was conducted in the middle of the night. Her body was guarded throughout by officers from Special Branch. An official photographer was brought in to document the minutiae of the proceedings. Such intimacies.

He was escorted to the lavatory, twice. He was searched upon entering the premises, and again when leaving. For what? A stashed film?

Too obvious.

They frisked him for a bit of hair. For a sample of body fluid. For a sacred scraping of DNA. They couldn't risk a tabloid relic. A black-market dream. A national security crisis.

When I eventually moved out of our little cottage, my old Kodak negatives of the long-ago day at the Hotel Nova Scotian fell out of an album, and I lifted them to the light of our bedroom window, peering.

5

Picture it.

'In my dream she'd been cremated,' said Patricia Garland of Manchester, after the news. 'And I had the urn, you know the safekeeping of the ashes, and the whole country knew. But my daughter Susannah spilled them all over the floor. I scooped them back into the urn as well as I could – I had to fool people – but I knew there were bits of stair carpet in there. It was awful. I woke myself up choking on the ash.'

6

The column inches were endless. I know because I bought every paper.

They killed her because she was dabbling in politics. Because she was turning to the Left. Because she had loose lips. Because she was about to marry an Arab. Because she was going to convert to Islam, like her friend Jemima Khan. Because she was carrying an illegitimate, Muslim baby. Because Charles could never otherwise have Camilla. Because he wanted Diana gone. Because she'd had the temerity to say he wanted her gone. Because Philip deemed it necessary. For the Monarchy, for the Firm. Because she was part of a psychic task-force and knew what They were up to.

Perhaps she wasn't the only one. Not long before her death, BBC journalists had practised in private a 'sudden and violent death scenario' – intended to cover travel accident, assassination or suicide – involving Diana, Princess of Wales.

On the BBC 1, she was Our Lady of Sorrows. On ITV, Diana the Martyred. On Sky TV, Diana the Goddess, spectacularly sacrificed.

On the night of the crash, just hours before her death, photos of the injured princess were valued at three hundred thousand pounds.

7

At the Pitié-Salpêtrière Hospital, as the sky lightened, Diana, Princess of Wales was pronounced dead from internal injuries.

In a nearby corridor where he'd waited through the night, the British Ambassador wept and wept like a child.

On hearing of her death, Shehnaz Shafi, 39, a Pakistani who had had his photo taken with the Princess the previous May in his village near Lahore, poisoned himself.

In Hong Kong, a young man jumped out of the thirty-third floor of a tower block. Cuttings about her death were found nearby.

When Jon woke me that morning with news of the unconfirmed reports, I lurched from sleep and sat upright. 'What?' I cried. I sped down the stairs to the TV.

After my teenage vigil at the Hotel Nova Scotian, I'd lost all interest in celebrity and royalty. I would have blushed to have been found reading a copy of *Hello* magazine. Yet the news on our television seemed to seep from the sad dream of our young marriage; from what a friend had once described to me as our slow car crash of a year.

That morning, on our rosy chintz sofa, I stood up often, switched channels and news programmes in search of the latest reports. I moved like a sleep-walker who is able to perform simple, mechanical tasks. Outside, Jon stood in the back garden, clearing the pond of the weed that had started to smell in the heat.

8

The day before the funeral, I told Jon I had a friend to see in London. I took the morning train to Victoria. On arrival, I stopped outside the station and selected a bouquet of miniature pink roses, although I hadn't planned on any such display.

My excuse was History. Later, on the phone, I would describe to my parents my position on the Royal Mile when the Union Flag was finally lowered over Buckingham Palace. I would conjure the scent of those seas of decaying blooms. My narration was childish – for my parents, I told myself. The Queen and the Duke had waved and smiled as they were driven into St James's Palace to view her body in the Chapel Royal. Yes, I said, the queue *was* endless. People came from all over the country to sign the books of condolence.

I didn't admit to anyone I'd tried, too late, to join that queue. As I stood near its end, I told myself: I didn't know the woman. It seemed important and merely decent to remain aware of that as assorted millions wept. I wasn't about to be confused with the mad and the sad.

But I *had* been drawn to the queue by repeated rumours of visions in the room where her body was resting. Even the *Independent* had reported the phenomenon. I wanted to join the queue fraudulently, simply to sneak a glimpse of the oil painting upon which Diana's face allegedly appeared. I wanted to witness for myself the collective dream.

Yet, as I hovered near the end of the queue, I realised it wasn't *Diana* those witnesses repeatedly described. Not her, but her picture: 'You know the pose,' one mourner told me. 'The picture with her head cupped in her hands. She's got the tiara on as well.'

Floating above a portrait of Charles I, above his right shoulder, was the image of Diana that had once appeared on the cover of *Vogue*. Mourners beheld, not the ghost of her, but the ghost of her image. Even in death, she was, it seems, reduced to it.

I phoned Jon from a payphone. I explained that the trains were slow. Standing room only. Everywhere I looked, people were unrolling sleeping bags and claiming their position on the funeral route. I stepped over pillows, candles and provisions. The crowd was profligate in its grief.

And it came to me then, the silly lover's test I'd once put to Jon years before. We'd been walking hand in hand, newly married, up the lane, past lambs and hedgerows. I'd grinned and tugged on his arm. 'If I were to die, would you marry again?'

He didn't laugh off the question or play the young hero and forswear the thought. He didn't insist I take the words back lest some pagan trickster god of the fields listened at that moment. Instead he pondered it. 'Yes,' he said thoughtfully. 'Yes, I suppose I would.'

9

'Is she real dead or pretend dead?' a small girl asked her mother as I walked away.

Princesses on biers usually open their eyes again.

In the underpass that night, she was found injured and semi-conscious, sitting in the footwell behind the driver's seat. When she was prised at last from the Mercedes and stretched out in the ambulance, a tear in a vein near her heart opened wide.

10

The CCTV footage from the Paris Ritz is time-stamped and as lifelike as an old flip-book. It should have been ephemera. It should have been 'wiped' in the way the hotel's security tapes were, routinely, each week. But here, she is alive once more, immortalised and moving in raw, stuttering frames.

First, rewind. Can you see? The camera on the Place Vendôme, at the front of the hotel, shows a legion of photographers and midnight onlookers who await her exit. Two decoy vehicles are ready, engines running.

On the recorder, the digital clock spins.

We move inside the Ritz now, into the foyer of her suite, and peer down like minor gods on Diana, her bodyguard, Dodi and the hotel escort. The floor is expensively tiled. They stand in a loose huddle. They confer. They nod. At seven minutes past twelve, they leave the suite. The four figures walk, in halting frames, to the service lift. She is tanned and her hair is very blonde with the sun and swimming of recent weeks. She has changed out of the linen trouser suit she arrived in that afternoon. She wears white capri trousers, a black scoop-necked top and black jacket.

As the doors of the lift close, she raises a chiding finger to Dodi, then laughs, covering her mouth like a mischievous schoolgirl. We don't hear the joke. Her bodyguard checks the details of the route in a pocket notebook.

Above them, out of time, I want to press rewind again, to spool the clock back. I want a maid, bearing a stack of fresh sheets, to hit the 'down' button, stumble into their world mid-descent and delay them with her apologies. I want her to bother Diana for a smile, a word, an autograph. I want her to alter the sequence.

On they go.

11

At seventeen minutes past twelve, Diana and Dodi are captured on CCTV in the corridor of the Ritz's service exit. Another lens. Their backs are turned to the camera's eye. A staff member is making notes against a glass-cabinet wall display – next week's laundry rota, let's say.

Dodi slips his left arm around Diana's back and pulls her close. His hand rests on her lower back, out of view (except for the camera's, that is, except for mine and yours). She slips her right arm behind herself and laces her fingers through his. No one can see, she tells herself. They wait. She leans, discreetly, against his chest and into his groin. His thumb moves up and down her spine.

At eighteen minutes past twelve, their driver arrives from the street. Diana releases Dodi's hand, straightens her jacket and gives her trousers a tug. His hand remains on her back. The driver steps into the street a final time to check the way is clear. She leans into Dodi again. The driver rejoins them to confirm the route they're about to take. At nineteen minutes past midnight, on the 31st of August 1997, they step into the rue Cambon.

12

Twelve hours later, at the bus shelter on my street, I hear someone talking: 'Everyone wants a piece of her.' Present tense, even then.

The paparazzi word for the hunt is 'monstering'. A few photographers, but only a few, make it to rue Cambon before her car speeds off. Picture the dismay of their faces, blurring in the windows of the black Mercedes sedan as it spirits her away from the Ritz that night. They're too late, she assures herself. They're running back for their motorbikes, but they're too late.

When the car departs, it is twenty past twelve.

Two and a half kilometres of life remain.

Three minutes.

Her pulse is fast. The car passes bright awnings, building skips and darkened balconies. As it emerges from the hushed backstreets, the city is a pointillist vision of lamplight against the midnight dark.

Fountains splash. Two minutes remain. The ancient obelisk at Place de la Concorde pierces the night. A green entrance to a Metro station is dim. Marble lions sleep above a street corner.

Ninety seconds.

Look. Don't look. Look.

Through the reinforced glass windows, the Seine rushes past. Diana turns and glances through the back window. The plan has worked. They've shaken the photographers. They've made their getaway. Paris by night is a live, radiant current, and in it, the river is shimmering, as if for her, when the sedan slips into the underpass beneath the Pont de l'Alma.

Her breath is slightly shallow. The night is close, humid, or so it feels to her. Her lover squeezes her hand. She thinks fleetingly about the cool, crisp linen of his bed; about the breeze that rises off the river and moves through his apartment. She is lulled momentarily by the memory of the slow-turning blades of the fan above his bed. Yes, she thinks, she is ready for sleep. She imagines her boys in their faraway beds, their brows sticky hot tonight. The cheek of her younger son is still velvet to the touch.

Twelve concrete pillars flicker past in quick succession. The exit is almost in sight when a white Fiat Uno appears (or doesn't appear) and clips (or doesn't clip) the Mercedes.

The Mercedes swerves catastrophically and slams into the thirteenth pillar at sixty-five miles per hour.

It spins and crashes again.

Thirteen pillars. Twelve quick frames. A fragile fragment of film. Or a strip of flimsy negatives, its images obscured. By the blur of high speed. By the smoke in the tunnel. By the skirmish of photographers who arrive minutes later. By the blitz of their flashbulbs and the emergency lights.

By fingerprints, countless. Long before. Long after.

By the uncanny double-exposure of our own private griefs.

13

In Praise of Radical Fish

Brothers, I tell you solemnly: it is not easy to become radicalised in a seaside resort. There are distractions. There are deckchairs. There is all that soft, watery light. What can a brother do but hope that the flame of his anger survives the refreshing sea breeze?

It was the Bank Holiday weekend, and I had coaxed Omar and Hamid to Brighton from Peterborough on the promise of a pre-jihad team-building weekend. If we could maintain our anger there, I told them, we could maintain it anywhere. Except I was the weak link. I still had to find the flame within. On Brighton Pier, while Omar and Hamid brooded like ayatollahs, I struggled with an embarrassing excess of good cheer. The day was bright, the tide was high. At the shooting gallery I managed to take out an entire row of ducks – only to spoil everything by returning to my brothers bearing cuddly toys.

Omar frowned. Hamid sighed. The *X Factor* buzzer sounded in my head.

Ham said, 'No one may hold a cuddly toy when the call to Holy War comes.'

'Ah,' I said. 'It is written?'

He and Omar exchanged a look. Ham knocked my head.

We were waiting for the call from the Emir's man on the Dark Web, aka The Recruiter. Hamid had acquired a second mobile purely for the purpose of the call, and it could, he said, come at any moment. If we were deemed proper, The Recruiter would tell us when and how to mobilise. He would get us maps, through a third party back in Peterborough, and a list of required kit.

Ahead of us, at the railing, a white guy vomited into the sea.

'Lim,' Hamid said to me, his voice public-school posh and low, 'listen. I am grateful for your efforts, I truly am, but' – he cast an eye over the pier – 'wouldn't a few lurid games of paintball in Peterborough have served? Brighton, I think, is a city of Kuffar. We should not be here.'

I was out of my depth when Muslims talked like Muslims. My father had always worked shifts and found it difficult to take me to mosque. I made a mental note to check the glossary in my *Islam for Dummies* – £12.40 RRP less my staff discount. Then I slapped Ham on the back and told him all would be well.

Omar also looked impressively miserable. How did they do it? I gathered the toys in my arms and assured them it would only strengthen us to confront and renounce the pleasures of Brighton. 'Watch,' I said.

The girl in the candyfloss booth was called Joy. It said so on her badge – only she had scratched out the 'y' in black biro.

'Did your boss get your name wrong?' I tried.

She was pretty even when she scowled.

'I'm Lim,' I added. 'As in Limazah.'

'I'm Jo,' she said. 'As in Jo.'

I smiled and arranged the toys, like supplicants, in a semicircle around her booth.

She rolled her eyes but laid down her flossy wand and stepped outside to see. 'I don't like it when customers use my real name.'

'Fair enough,' I said.

She beheld the many lopsided smiles, then bent down and tentatively stroked a furry blue dolphin. In the light of day, her skin and hair sparkled with a fine residue of spun sugar. 'You're nice,' she said.

Nice? *Nice?* If only she knew. With any luck, by the following week, I'd be sporting a Kalashnikov and the unattractive early growth of a hard-core beard.

Her nose stud twinkled in the midday sun. 'Here.' She took my phone from my shirt pocket and typed her number in. Then, in a moment's afterthought, she added her name.

Three taps.

I couldn't help myself. I punched the air.

'Bye, Limazah,' she said, smiling shyly and returning to her temple.

'Bye, Joy,' I said, and I walked-the-walk back to Omar and Hamid.

If anything, their superior anger had only improved in my absence.

'What was that white girl doing with your phone?' asked Hamid.

I laid my hand on his shoulder. 'Most worthy brother,' I said, 'I take my balaclava off to you. I really do. You are a gentleman and a scholar. You know what to be angry about. I can only follow your lead. That's why we're here. To learn. To be tested. We must think of Brighton as the Endurance Course of the Soul.'

'Did you endure?' he asked.

'No,' I confessed.

He sighed again.

Hamid, a student of Islamic philosophy, had never travelled farther south than London, while Omar had never seen the sea except on telly. We'd met earlier that year at the Gladstone Street mosque in Peterborough and were all nineteen. Omar was unemployed, even though his father was big in dried fruits – Turkish apricots, figs, dates, sultanas, prunes. Omar and his old man had fallen out when Omar announced he'd rather die than follow in his father's footsteps.

Die?

His father had laughed and mocked, and as he did, the words spilled uncontrollably from Omar's mouth: 'Yes, *die!* I will go to the Land of Honour.'

'Ha!' His father started shouting wildly in Turkish. 'You think they will want you? With the amount you sleep? With the amount you eat? *Ha!* Do you imagine they will keep you in hair gel? But if it's jihad you want—'

'I will make plans,' Omar bluffed. 'You'll see.'

'—then it's jihad you get.' His father walked to his desktop, pushed aside a sticky bowl of prunes, clicked on easyJet reservations and opened a Google map of Turkey. 'Here,' he said, his blunt finger stabbing the screen. 'Cross at Bab al-Hawa. Pack a compass. Don't eat with your left hand. Don't show anyone the soles of your feet. And send your mother a postcard.' Then he clicked once, twice, three times, and Omar's one-way ticket was booked.

I found him prostrate and trembling in the prayer room on Gladstone Street. 'Listen, bro,' I said, 'you might *not* die. I mean, like, really. I don't think martyr-dom is strictly required.' I racked my brain. 'Besides, on Twitter, they're saying it's five-star out there.' I slid my phone from my pocket and got down on my haunches. 'Look at these pix. They've got Red Bull and KitKats, and shiny new PlayStations. I tell you, it's Jannah on earth, man. And OK, if it gets too intense, think Plan B: Ahmed, that guy who works Saturdays at Thomas Cook, says that conflict tourism is the next big thing. Omar, bro, adventure here you come.' I whistled. 'I'm jealous. Like, really.'

He looked up at me with the eyes of an abandoned child. 'So you want to come too? You mean it?'

My words dried up. My tongue wouldn't work. For a moment, I could only rock on my heels and scratch my head. What had I done? Was I a true friend or wasn't I? Was I a brother? Finally I shrugged. 'Like, yeah, OK, why not? Hamid's on his way. Why not us? Christ, yeah.'

Omar was so relieved he didn't even tell me off for swearing in C. of E.

Hamid was an altogether different case. He was pure of heart, the idealist among us. He had dropped out of university in London when he'd discovered the campus was – as he described it – 'a hotbed of liberal consensus'. Whatever that was when it was at home. 'Alas,' said Hamid, 'I would have learned more about Holy War in a squalid backstreet Internet café in Peterborough.' *Why*, he wondered, weren't Muslims rushing to defend the lives of other Muslims?

I reminded him that, in the Land of Honour, he would have to avoid words like 'alas' and 'squalid' if he wanted to make a good first impression and not have a plastic bag forced over his head and tied at the neck on Day One. He nodded. Hamid was posh, not stupid.

We had three tickets left for the pier. On the ghost train, our carriage tipped and skidded through the darkness. Skulls flew past and severed arms reached out to grab us, but we maintained our hard-man faces, no problem. Then, out of nowhere, three headless horsemen bore down on us, like the Janjaweed out of Sudan, and we hurtled deeper into the underworld.

I have to be honest: the sound of screaming was my own.

There is much to overcome.

Take the nudist beach that afternoon.

We had positioned ourselves, clothed and vigilant, at the beach's western boundary. The sun hammered down, and we passed a bottle of water between us. The point of the exercise was, I explained, to learn to harden ourselves to scenes of Western decadence.

With hindsight, naturally, I blame myself. But there and then, Hamid nodded. He liked a spiritual test. A scene of so much exposed flesh was, he said, an affront to all that was holy and good. Omar was less high-minded. He shuddered at the evidence of what age and gravity can do to a body. I proposed that we remain in position on the beach until we had observed at least one beautiful naked woman. Could we overcome our lust? That, I said, was our sacred challenge, and I, for one, embraced it.

They each nodded. Hamid checked his phone to make sure we hadn't missed The Call. Then he switched on the camera, and, with an outstretched, rigid arm, held the zoom at the ready. 'Good man,

Hamid,' I said, clapping him on the back. When the moment came, we would not spare ourselves a single detail.

But the woman never appeared. In Brighton it seemed only families, gay men and old people took off their clothes. To make matters worse, Omar kept leaving desperate voicemails for his mother to ask if his father had backed down yet. When he called again, his old man picked up.

As I say, I blame myself. But if Omar hadn't started shouting, itemising for the benefit of his father's moral outrage the jihadi excesses he would perpetrate in the family's name, we might not have had to run like maniacs from the three coppers who laid siege following complaints from the public. Before we had the chance to harden ourselves to even one naked female, they gave chase.

While Hamid had the purity of heart and Omar, his father's business brain, I had the reaction time and speed, even, it seemed, on beach pebbles. Back in Peterborough, I walked ten hours a night across the Amazon warehouse – otherwise known as the Fulfilment Centre. The Centre is the size of seven football pitches, and my average pick-rate was one product every twenty-nine seconds. Even as I speak, the proof is on the warehouse wall, in a Black Maxi Shatter-proof Poster Frame, RRP £19.99. My 'Employee of the Month' picture.

Everyone there calls me 'Legs' because 1) I *am* fast and 2) no white person can ever remember 'Limazah'. Joy was the first.

I never knew it till the day Omar asked me to flee with him to jihad, but I wanted to know what fulfilment meant when Amazon wasn't number-crunching the shit out of it.

At the police station, Omar and Ham weren't detained for more than a few hours, but they were cautioned for public disturbance, and now were known to the police. It was difficult to say how much the cops knew about Omar's jihadi boasts to his father, but the truth was, he'd been giving it large there on the beach.

Those few hours alone were not easy for me either. Would Omar and Ham be released? Were the cops still looking for me? Had they seized Hamid's phone? Had The Recruiter made contact even as they sat in the interview room?

Perhaps it was the trance of the surf, or maybe the sweet smell of suncream, but when Omar and Ham finally returned, I clasped each to my chest in a spontaneous show of happiness and brotherly love.

Omar frowned. Hamid sighed. Where was my righteous anger?

The *X Factor* buzzer sounded again.

Then Omar's phone rang and we jumped. It was Omar's mother. His father, she told him, hadn't relented. Omar could only return home to pack a bag for Turkey.

'Tell the old prune I can't wait to go!' he said. But as he ended the call, he had to wipe his eyes with the back of his hand.

'No, no, no,' I counselled as his knees gave way and he sank to my beach towel. 'Hold on to your anger, bro. In the days to come, it will sustain you when your feet are blisters, when your eyes are blind with sand and when you're cursing yourself for having an iPod in your pocket instead of toilet paper.'

Hamid was angrier and more committed than ever. Another neighbourhood in his parents' native city had been flattened that very morning. Plus, he added, the tea in the police station had been of the poorest variety and quite frankly, an insult. Did the English working classes *strive* to be common?

Back on the prom, we spotted CCTV everywhere. At last, even my cheer faltered. Were we now being watched? 'Brothers,' I said, 'we need to disappear.'

'We need to get our arses underground,' said Omar.

'We need a phone signal,' said Hamid.

Because everything still depended on that call.

'The *Sea Life* Centre?' said Omar.

As if he could do better.

'*Think*,' I said. 'How often do you see coppers out enjoying a family attraction?' Omar and Ham strained to recall. Earnestness, I feared, would be our undoing.

'Go, go, go!' I ordered, and we sped down the concrete stairs, with Ham pulling up the rear.

A welcome sign said that the Aquarium had been enjoyed by families since 1871. Omar said they must have been, like, really, really bored in the olden days. There, beneath the coast road, the Sea Life Centre stretched out before us in vaulted Victorian gloom. The air was humid. The lights were dim. The tanks gleamed. I took a deep breath. 'Try to look normal,' I whispered. 'Try to blend in.'

'With fucking *fish*?' asked Omar.

The place was packed and noisy with Bank Holiday families. Perfect. My heart stopped thudding. We slid through the cavern of the public hall, past the snack stand, and started to relax at last. There was no sign of Security, no one with bad-ass flaks or Bluetooth.

So we pressed our faces to the tanks and became schoolboys all over again. We had time to kill, didn't we? Omar and I made kissy fish-lips at assorted occupants of the tanks, and even Hamid laughed because, *man*, some of those fish were big ugly sons-of.

'Ham,' I said, 'check. How many bars on the phone?'

'Three,' he said.

'*Result*,' I said.

Children's voices bounced off stone walls and pillars. At the rock pool, we stirred up the starfish and prodded the crabs. I walked sideways for a time, for a laugh. But I admit: something deep in my gut wobbled when a hairy mofo of a catfish looked me in the eye. I knew it and it knew it too: a primitive, unspeakable understanding was hurdling the space between its brain and mine.

We were each capable of ugly things.

'This way!' I said, waving us forward and deeper.

And deeper still — past tanks of pulsating jellyfish and pale electric eels. We stood, watching the eels slide between red fingers of coral. 'Ham,' I called over my shoulder, 'how many bars now?'

'Two!'

Up ahead, an octopus writhed, all arms and suckers. 'Allah made a mistake with that one,' I laughed.

Hamid boxed my ears.

Which is when we turned a tight corner and it appeared: a shining glass tunnel of water and light.

'*Allahu Akbar*,' whispered Ham.

It was beautiful — beautiful like nothing I've ever known in Peterborough. Beautiful like it would be on the inside of one of those snow-domes, only with fish floating past instead of snow. I suddenly felt small, small like a barnacle stuck to the rock of the world. But if I was that small it was because the world was big and, *inshallah*, eternal. A crazy kind of calm washed over me, and there, underground and on the run, I felt my heart lift.

We stepped inside the tunnel, pointing and gawping. Light pulsed across the glass, and it morphed from soft purple to blue to green. Enormous sea turtles paddled by. Sharks hovered overhead like guardians. Stingrays zipped and glided. Streams of bubbles rose up and, as we walked on, a bower of angelfish and butterflyfish moved with us.

All was one there, underground. There were no borders. No walls or checkpoints. No them, no us.

Omar's mouth gaped. His eyes shone. Ham shuffled forward, staring at the pure white bellies of the sharks overhead. Classical music dripped from the walls. I thought, it's like that tunnel they say appears when you die.

Which is when Omar's phone bleeped and he fumbled for it. 'What the f—'

I eyeballed him. We couldn't risk complaints.

'I don't believe it,' he said, blinking back tears and grinning all at once. 'It's a text from my mother. It was a big wind-up. My father wanted to teach me a lesson. I'm flying to Turkey next week to oversee a shipment of dates.' He raised his eyes to the bright glassy sky and gave thanks. '*Dates!*'

'Bro,' I said, 'I'm really, really happy for you. Like, really.' And OK, maybe I was happy for myself too. Cos, as of that moment, I was off – the – hook. A free fish.

Hamid, devout radical though he was, clapped Omar on the back. It was big of him. A shoal of Boy Scouts moved past, their chatter briefly deafening. Then the hush returned to the tunnel and we heard the ringtone of Hamid's phone.

da nuh
da nuh
da nuh da nuh da nuh da nuh

The theme from *Jaws.*
Hamid froze. Omar and I froze. Even the shark overhead froze.
We looked at the display. 'It's him,' said Ham.
The Emir's man.
We stared for long moments at the throbbing screen. A baby sea turtle swam up to the glass and stared too.
Then Hamid swallowed hard and, with one gentle swipe of the finger, ended the call.
'The Moving Finger writes,' he said,

'and having writ,
Moves on: nor all your Piety nor Wit
Shall lure it back to cancel half a Line.'

'An old Persian poem,' he murmured.
Omar stood blinking, dazed with relief. I seized Hamid's head between my hands and kissed it hard. In the water above us, a troop of striped clownfish bounced in the current.
And moments later, as we stepped up into the soft light of evening, I suddenly remembered Joy.

Imagining Chekhov

Woman with Little Pug

From *Murray's Handbook for Travellers in Russia* (1868): 'The numbers going to bathe at Yalta bid fair to make it the new Russian Brighton.'

At the Grand Hotel in Brighton, the appearance of a new arrival – a woman with a little dog – became the general topic of conversation amongst the front-desk staff and regulars. Guy Ingram, seated in the conservatory with the morning paper on his knee, observed her approach the vast zinc dais of the hotel bar, push back her floppy hat and ask the bartender for a bowl of water for her pug pup.

In the days that followed, Guy glimpsed the woman on the prom, in the Pavilion gardens and in the twisting, tourist-mobbed Lanes. She was invariably alone and wearing the same straw hat with a pair of oversized dark glasses. The pug trotted along after her, in tow on its silver lead. On occasion it lay cradled in her arms, its legs – Guy sickened at the sight – grotesquely akimbo.

Guy had recently passed the crumbling milestone that is one's fiftieth year. He had a ten-year-old daughter, Hermione, and twin sons, Seb and Julian, who had gone off to board at the age of twelve. It was unnatural, he'd insisted to his wife, for boys to kick about the house after they'd reached puberty. He'd reminded her that he had boarded from the tender age of eight, when his parents had turfed him out, and had it done *him* any harm? Was *he* emotionally stunted?

Four years his senior, Martha's most recent midlife crisis was a Master's course in Psychodynamic Therapy. She passed entire days in the breakfast room making masks with old greeting cards, glitter, feathers, condoms and the burst blister packs from her antidepressants. What did it mean? Guy asked himself, but never for long.

His own midlife crisis – if 'crisis' was indeed the right word – had manifested itself in a series of extramarital dalliances arranged online. After a few brief encounters, he'd quickly determined that the most efficacious way past a woman's guilt or unease was an unshowy display of calculated compassion. It was no longer helpful to say, 'My wife is prone to headaches', as it had been for the cavorting class of his father's generation. No, these days one explained with an air of utter decency and restrained grief: 'My wife suffers from depression.'

The opportunities seemed endless. Just last month, he'd popped down to Brighton, ostensibly for an appointment with Roedean's headmistress to discuss Hermione's chances. He'd explained to Martha that the head's day for meeting parents was Wednesday – Martha's MA workshop day.

Pity.

This week, his escapades in Brighton doubled as a search for investment properties. It was a bonus that the pert, young estate agent had warmed to his financial savvy. In truth, knowledge of the market and its vagaries constituted little more than ball-scratching for a City man of his calibre. But Gemma might merit more. She'd worn a prim navy dress, a beguiling trench coat and knocked-off Louboutins.

The louche morality of Brighton was of course overstated; that particular version of the town existed mostly in the febrile imaginations of middle-aged, soft-paunched Londoners who longed to have more than A level results and the fear of mansion tax to occupy their Dark Nights of the Soul. That said, he was happy enough to succumb to seaside cliché. It was really rather fun.

Ascending the spiral staircase to his room, he tapped his breast pocket for Gemma's card. Overhead, the Grand's vast cupola ennobled him. It made him feel *not*-sordid, and he never failed to appreciate the crowning view. Except now, as Guy turned his eyes skyward, he experienced something strange, something alien – a sharp and repeated sense of loss – for above him, disappearing again and again at each bend in the spiral, was the woman in the floppy hat.

A few hours later, Guy predicted – correctly – that the woman would be too besotted to leave the dog behind in her room at dinner time; instead she would ask for a plate of something to be served to her in the conservatory. The evening was sultry, and he had already taken up his position when she walked languidly in, the pug scampering after her, its claws clattering horribly on the tiles. Tat-a-tat-tat.

Through the wide windows, the Channel was glassy. The gulls cried out. The full moon was a stopped pendulum, grave and low above the sea. There wasn't a breath of a breeze or a single white-cap.

The woman slipped off her hat and laid it by her feet before turning to take in the view. In the deep twilight, the ribbed ruins of the West Pier dissolved into shadow.

When the waiter appeared, Guy assured him that he was quite happy to eat his leg of lamb from a tray. It wouldn't be a problem. After all, the temperature was more pleasant in the conservatory.

Whether the pug growled at him, the waiter or them both, it was impossible to say.

Guy ordered baby carrots and potato gratin but resisted the caramelised onion gravy. He chose a 2005 red Bordeaux, sank deeper into his armchair and remembered the sensation of closing his father's eyelids after the old man had emptied of life. On the pillow below him, the bald, freckled dome of the paternal head had suddenly looked too small.

He watched the woman shake out a napkin and bend to wipe the pug's nose. An errant slant of light from a colonial shutter fell across her face. The band on her ring finger glinted.

Guy's meal arrived. He listened to her order the *soupe du jour* and a glass of Sancerre, to be charged to her room. 'Six-three-four,' she confirmed in a low, resonant voice. He repeated it to himself, and only now, as she shifted in her seat, did he see that she was actually far less beautiful than he'd imagined. Her hair was a faded brown; her eyes, an indistinct grey. Her cleavage turned faintly crêpe-like as she bent to stroke the dog. She was older than her slim figure suggested. Quite unremarkable in fact. Yet she intrigued him and he had no idea why.

He caught her eye, nodded and, as if on a whim, asked if he might offer the pug a morsel of lamb.

The woman looked up at him and immediately lowered her eyes. 'He doesn't bite,' she said, blushing.

The pug sucked the lamb from his fingers. Revolting. 'How long have you been visiting?' he asked, as if summoning polite interest.

'A couple of days. My husband was supposed to join me. We won this week at the Grand at his office Christmas party last year. But he's been delayed.'

Her wine arrived. The waiter receded. For a long moment neither spoke.

'I'm supposed to be enjoying myself,' she said, smiling unhappily, 'but the truth is I'm bored.' She blinked several times, as if she would blink away the words.

And again he saw his father's dead, bewildered eyes asking, *Is that all?*

It was agreed with the peculiar ease of the mildly inebriated. He waited in the lobby while she returned the pug to her room. Room 634, he reminded himself. They crossed the King's Road, making a mad dash through traffic. On the beach, she grabbed hold of his arm so as not to topple in her wedges. The pebbles crunched underfoot. It was the last Bank Holiday weekend of summer and the shingle was littered with drunken, furtive couples.

Guy and Anna seated themselves on his jacket. They noted how warm it was still, even at midnight. Guy told her that he worked in the City; that he owned two homes in London but was in search of investment properties in Brighton. He said that, once upon a time, he used to act – on stage, that is – revues, comedies – at Cambridge, but that person seemed like a distant relation now. Anna said she'd grown up in London but lived in Surrey. Her husband was away a great deal in Asia. His company sold health insurance to expats. He had trouble with his eyes. Her only talent was the piano. She was good but not gifted. 'No,' she said, 'no children.'

He took her hand in his and when she did not withdraw it, something tripped in his brain. The moon seemed to sway. The pendulum swung.

'You seem oddly familiar,' she said.

'More familiar than odd, I hope.' And he did. He did hope.

They watched a satellite cross the night sky, a lonely pinprick of light.

He unbuttoned his shirt and laid his head in her lap. She fingered the hair of his chest. He forgot that he was a philanderer, a player, a user of women; forgot that he had often been here – or somewhere very like it – before. In that moment, absolved by the hushing of the tide, each foundered inwardly.

Later, as they walked through the door into Anna's room, her hand shot to her mouth. 'My dog . . . Oh, god. Where is he?' She searched the bathroom. She peered under the bed and beneath the writing desk, coaxing and cooing. She ransacked the suitcase on the floor. Guy drew back the curtains. He even opened the wardrobe. But the pug pup was nowhere, and indeed there was no evidence it ever had been. 'His bowl was here,' she tried. 'His lead was by the minibar. I can't believe it! Someone's taken him!'

Guy also couldn't believe it. He was first to realise. 'Anna, sit down.'

'There was a squeaky toy,' she explained. 'A fat toy mouse. They've even taken that!'

'Anna ...'

'I'll ring Reception,' she said, her eyes tearing up.

'No ...' How to say it? 'There's no need.'

'Of course there is! They might have CCTV—'

'No. Listen to me. There's no need' – he took a deep breath – 'because *there is no dog.*'

'What do you mean, there's no dog? Of course there's a—' She lowered herself stiffly to the edge of the bed.

'Come on now. You know it too ... You know you do. The dog was only ever a ... a device. A contrivance.'

'Don't say that! He was here just a few—'

'Think about it. You were so remote. What else would have allowed me to approach? We needed the eponymous dog.'

She blinked several times. Then she pressed her hands to her face. 'Dear God. I can't even tell you his name.'

'Because there never was a name.'

'But he's all I had.'

'That's not true. You're upset. You only need—'

'Lord. He *is* gone, isn't he?'

'For now at least.'

'And we're next, aren't we? You and me.'

'Let me get you a glass of water.'

She caught hold of his hand. 'Stories are dreadful things. You know that, don't you?' She looked about the room, then kicked open her suitcase. 'Let's run. Please. Let's get out of here while we can. Let's get a cab, a train, a steamer—' She looked up at him, horrified. 'Did you *hear* what I just said? *A steamer* ... That's Yalta. I hardly even know where Yalta is, but some ... some bit of me does ... dimly.' Her face went pale. 'There's no time, is there?'

'Listen.' He rubbed her back. 'We'll go everywhere. The prom, the Pier. We'll walk along the undercliff. We'll have a perfect time.' He unbuttoned her blouse and kissed her shoulder. 'You'll ride the carousel. We'll lounge on the beach and have ice cream in the Gardens. On Ship Street, we'll stand and listen to the piano player in the eyepatch and waistcoat. We'll climb high on the Downs and look over an impossibly blue sea, a village church, on wheat blazing gold in the last of the day's light. You'll say—'

'"There's dew on the grass."'

'And I'll say, "Time to go home."'

'As if we *have* a home . . .' Her voice trailed away.

'Yes . . .' He caught sight of himself in the mirror on the wall. 'As if . . .' Christ, when had he turned so grey?

'And when there is no one in sight—' she began.

'—I will draw you to me and kiss you passionately.'

'But I'm no one,' she said. 'A Home Counties wife. A faithless one at that. Before the end of our week, I'll loathe myself and I'll bore you. You'll be relieved when it comes to an end.'

'Only because I always am.'

'Which makes me even more ridiculous. Yet I'll cry when you see me off at the station.' A reluctant smile got hold of her lips. '*Without* my lapdog in my lap.'

He laughed. 'Without your *nameless* lapdog in your lap.'

'We'll smell autumn in the air, won't we?'

'Don't think of that now.'

'You'll go home to your family.'

'And you to your husband. It's fate, I suppose, or something like.'

148

'I don't love him but I can't leave him. He has a condition. His eyes. In a few years, he'll be mostly blind. In any case, you'll be at it online in no time. Ashley Bloody Madison, or the next adultery site *du jour*.'

'But I won't be able to shake you from my thoughts. I'll catch a train to Redhill. Often. I'll watch your house. I'll go half-mad with the ache of you.'

She buried her face in his chest. 'I just want *to live!*'

'One night, I'll follow you and your husband to a restaurant on the high street. A sushi bar.'

'The Geisha Girl,' she said. 'Yes . . . I know it.'

'I'll motion you outside.'

'Already I feel sick.'

'And that will be the start—'

'I will have tried *so hard* to forget you.'

'—the start of our real life. Of a life so real we'll steal it like thieves if we have to.'

'We're ruined,' she whispered.

'Better secrecy and ruin than despair.'

At the window, the thin curtains lifted – although there was no breeze at all. Guy drew Anna close, and they stared into the night. The sea was black. The sky was black. All the lights on the Pier had gone out. Even the full moon had been extinguished from the fictive sky.

'There's hardly any time,' she murmured.

Beneath his hands, her shoulders started to quiver.

'Lie down,' he said, his voice hoarse with tenderness.

Chekhov's Telescope

On the deck of the *Alexander II*, Anton Pavlovich Chekhov looked up as the siren sounded. Overhead, the funnels puffed uselessly. In the bay, at swimming distance from shore, the steamer had run aground in just three feet of water.

Most of the holidaymakers retreated to the refreshment bar for complimentary smoked sausage and beer. The steamer's captain shouted at the band, which struck up a brassy tune. Only Anton Chekhov, Olga Knipper and assorted children remained at the rails, staring into the green, transparent sea of Yalta. At the captain's order, two sailors stripped naked and dived overboard to investigate the hull. A woman with bulging eyes and a stubborn pout emerged from the bar to tut at the sight of buttocks flying in First Class. Anton leaned into Olga: 'That one has gills beneath her stays,' he whispered, and Olga buried her grin in his chest.

From a pocket Chekhov produced a small naval telescope, extended it and passed it to her. 'Tell me what you see, dear actress.'

She pressed it to her eye. 'Mountains that hug the bay!'

He turned her body twenty degrees to the right. 'There. What do you see now?'

'A wasteland, with three half-dead fruit trees.'

He sighed, took the telescope and rubbed the eyepiece with his cuff. 'Come, come. This thing was dear. It sees through *time* as well as space. Now look again. There is a clearing. In the clearing is a dacha, a white dacha. Three storeys high with many windows and at least two balconies. You can't miss it.'

'Ah! The sun was in my eyes.'

'Can you see the garden? So many different kinds of roses! Tulips of every colour. Hyacinths. A mulberry tree. Cedars. A willow. Plus an orchard of cherry trees, and long, winding paths.'

'Excellent for your pacing.'

'What else can you spot?'

'Indoors . . . a piano. A generous table. Many guests.' She raised her eyebrows. 'And *so* many women at the windows! Devoted readers, assorted actresses, alluring acolytes, converted sapphists, young virgins and miscellaneous prostitutes – all with their faces pressed to the glass!'

He grabbed the telescope. 'On the contrary, I see a private room. The bed is exceedingly narrow. Practically monastic. It's a blessing I can't seem to put on weight or I would roll out of it each night.'

'How then do you accommodate the women? Do you have a stacking system?'

'Forget the bedroom – though, naturally, dear Olya, I hope you won't. Look instead into the window of the study. The large picture window.'

'Yes . . . I see your desk with your pen and . . . a new manuscript. A love story. An unexpected love story, I think. The story of a philanderer's redemption. The woman, however, is, I believe, quite ordinary.'

He frowned. 'They sound like unpromising characters. Besides, I haven't written anything in a year.'

'I see its pages as we speak. Next to it on the desk is your stethoscope, your little doctor's hammer and a bowl of calling cards.'

'And do you see a man there at the window?'

'Indeed. He is tall and cuts a handsome figure.'

'What is he doing?'

'Watching us through a telescope of course – and wondering who those two happy characters are on the toppled steamer.'

'Poor miserable wretch. He's stuck on that hillside, alone and heartsick.'

'Has he foundered in the manner of our steamer?'

'He has, I believe. But we must hope that he is not beyond salvation.' And in spite of the sailors and the children on deck, Anton Chekhov pressed Olga's palm to his lips even as two stout tugs drew alongside the *Alexander II*, ready to haul all souls back into the current.

The *Crimean Courier* was the first paper to announce the return of Russia's celebrated writer to Yalta. The reporter, a raw-faced youth called Sergei, studied Anton Chekhov as he descended the gangway, noting that the Great Man was thinner than when he had departed the town, and oddly pale at the height of summer. The woman was some ten years younger – thirty perhaps – with brown hair, an eager smile, small eyes and incipient jowls. Later, his editor, would strike out this detail, informing Sergei that the news – the *story* – was the arrival of Yalta's most famous bachelor with a woman on his arm, a leading actress of the Moscow Art Theatre.

'And what of the facts?' asked Sergei, his face reddening.

'The facts must fit the story,' said the editor, cuffing him. 'Only stories are true in the end. Especially in Russia.'

Sergei rubbed his cheek. What nonsense old people spoke.

From the landing stage, he watched the writer pause at the top of the gangway and breathe deeply.

'This air! So good for your lungs!' Olga declaimed.

'If only my lungs could live in Yalta,' grumbled Chekhov, 'and let me return to Moscow. I wouldn't even mind if they ran up expenses. They could stroll the promenade, go to the theatre and play cards.' He stared down the gangway. 'Lo! I believe this is what is known as the Long Slow Decline.'

'Anyone would think you were approaching seventy, not forty.'

'My haemorrhoids, dear Olya, would agree.'

'Now I know why women swoon.'

He smiled shyly, threw back his shoulders and offered her his arm.

Sergei Rogov had a ruthless eye, long legs and his quarry in view.

He followed the Great Writer, first to the genteel home of Dr Sredin, where Chekhov had arranged lodgings for Olga, so that she, an actress, might appear respectable during her stay in Yalta. Such hypocrisy, thought Sergei. Nearby, Chekhov booked himself into a balcony room on the third floor of the Hotel Marino.

The youth had waited on a bench opposite the hotel for five hours, sustaining himself on cured sturgeon and day-old bread, when his efforts were at last rewarded. A carriage drew up and Olga stepped out, her head bowed. Oh, the elaborate ruses of the middle-aged, thought Sergei, spitting out his crusts.

Late the next morning, at his lookout once more, he intercepted a note Chekhov had entrusted to an illiterate porter. The man was to deliver it to Dr Sredin's home, but Sergei gave the man a rouble and quickly copied it into his notebook.

Dear ravishing actress, good day! How is life with you? How are you feeling? I am writing in a corner of my bedroom. Our mouse is still here and happy. It likes my shoes. I will meet you at noon. Big, big kisses. 400 of them.

A libertine, thought Sergei.

He followed the lovers along the broad promenade, through the town park and up the hillside to Autka, where Chekhov was overseeing the construction of an oversized house for himself. Later, the young reporter hired a horse and followed their carriage at a stealthy distance up the pine-forested hillside to Oreanda, where he and said horse took cover behind the church as the pair reclined, overlooking the Bay. On the descent, however, Sergei was brought up short and nearly exposed when Chekhov's hand rapped suddenly on the carriage roof. In the woods, writer and actress disappeared behind a derelict hunting lodge and laughed so hard that the Great Writer had to halt in his exertions to let a coughing fit pass.

Sergei checked his fob watch. He recorded the duration of the lovemaking in his notebook.

Twelve minutes.

Olga's skin was very white.

The following morning, the lazy porter crossed the street, demanded two roubles and hand-delivered the note to Sergei. Once more Sergei copied it out, folded it and returned it to the man.

My glorious actress, I could run across a field in pure idiot delight, through the wood, across a stream and over several sheep. Try not to be bored at the table of the good doctor. I will work this morning on the story – the peculiar love story you foresaw, and set in Yalta no less. I will come to you after lunch. Thin though you say I am, do not underestimate me. At your earliest convenience I will love you wildly. Your Antoine.

From the veranda of the doctor's home, Chekhov hailed a landau to take them to the Imperial Palace. Sergei followed behind in a tourists' omnibus and closed in on his prey in an Italianate courtyard. He noted that the Great Writer wore grey trousers and that his jacket was blue and too short. Fact.

Olga sang a tune.

Fact.

They ate a picnic of pastries.

Fact.

That evening, Chekhov joined Olga, Dr Sredin, his wife, her sister and brother-in-law for dinner. Afterwards, croquet was played in the garden. Sergei watched through a gap in the box hedge. Dr Sredin and Chekhov joked disrespectfully about the incompetence of the local authorities. Sergei recorded each affront. They criticised the government's treatment of the local Tatar population, and Sergei scribbled every unwise word. The others retired indoors but the doctor and doctor–writer whacked the wooden balls until long after sunset, striking matches to see by until – Sergei consulted his watch – ten minutes past ten.

The idle rich.

But the following day, Sergei's cover was nearly blown. He looked up from his notebook outside the Hotel Marino only to see Chekhov, on his balcony with his notebook and pen in hand, observing *him*. The young spy departed his bench, almost running from the scene. But as he slowed to a walk, he couldn't help but wonder what Chekhov the Great Writer might have written about him, and his heart fluttered.

His assignment, however, was not complete. He tracked Chekhov and Olga to the road that climbed out of Yalta towards Ai-Petri, 4,000 feet above sea level. They travelled on foot, past sheep, goats and ancient wells, en route to the famous waterfall below the peak. Chekhov carried their rucksack of provisions. The road was sun-baked and he stopped often, bending to breathe. Olga remonstrated. She wanted to carry the rucksack. Chekhov shouted back. He was a doctor, wasn't he, and perfectly qualified to judge whether he was or was not able to walk to a local beauty spot. Sergei could almost taste the headline. 'Public Altercation Between Great Writer and Paramour'. He watched the actress return alone down the dusty road without a backward glance.

Sergei was already celebrating his forthcoming byline with vodka and *tchibureks* when he spotted the illiterate porter from the Hotel Marino. The man was walking in the direction of Dr Sredin's house. Sergei lowered his face. In truth, he did not want another instalment. He had story enough. But the porter had spotted him.

'Three roubles,' he demanded gloomily.

What could Sergei do? The man was lazy but looked very strong. He sighed and handed the money over.

My dearest Olya, forgive me. You see, I have this flu I can't quite shake. I am frustrated with <u>myself</u>, not you. You know I am forbidden another Moscow winter, and I fear that, 800 miles from here, you'll forget who I am. So my mood at times is parched and black, like the Crimean soil. Don't be angry with me, my darling. Our mouse is well and tolerates my temper. It asks to be remembered to you. Please reconsider and let me take you to G— this evening. The water will be bliss for your bathing, if too cold for this wretch. I will sit on the rocks and behold you. I kiss you and hug you. Your Antonio.

Sergei discovered the pair in the cove at Gurzov that evening, and as he hid behind a conveniently positioned outcrop of rock, his headline receded over the horizon. He despaired at the sight of Olga paddling happily in her underclothes and Chekhov fishing from the rocks. Ahead, in a rocky corner, dolphins herded mackerel, the arcs of their backs flashing silver. Olga pointed and clapped.

Sergei wanted to object. Did they not realise? There was no story in happiness!

How he despised those who had all the good fortune in this world. How he loathed their holiday fun. When had he ever been granted a day's holiday by his brute of an editor? When would he not have to buy day-old bread? When might he impress a woman enough to love him?

'I'll be lucky,' Chekhov called to Olga, 'if the dolphins spare me a single mackerel!'

'I shall swim out and tell the big ones you're over here.'

'It does not matter, dear Olya, whether they are big or small. I am simply grateful for a fish, as I am for any fish of an idea for a story. I never think, this is a big fish or little fish, a big idea or small idea. One does not know what will surface. One learns only to receive.'

She slipped beneath the waves and bobbed up below him, grabbing hold of his pole and shaking the end so its little bell rang.

'Well, what a catch,' he declared, laughing. 'If I may say, *you're* no mackerel or mullet.'

'Say you love me – or I won't let go of your pole.'

'I live in earnest hope.'

Behind his rock, Sergei, curiously, found himself grinning with Chekhov. He'd last grinned four years before when he saw a three-legged dog gambolling down the prom. His grin was not his own, but Chekhov's grin. His delight was Olga's delight. Their story was overtaking him. He experienced a buzzing lightness at his core, as if he were no longer flesh and bone; no longer an alert intelligence crashing about in a tall, angular body. Writing was fishing. Fishing was writing. The world was made of riddles, not facts. Chekhov had caught love at the end of his line. The backs of the dolphins were there and gone. Below the waterline, the mackerel schooled and scattered. From the waves, Olga told Chekhov that acting was not acting, but *being*. Her hair was loose behind her. In the water, she shone. She stood up and fell down again, laughing. Chekhov laid down his pole and scrambled like a boy from his perch. He crossed the pale shingle, his shoes soaked by the tide, and gathered her in his arms. Water streamed down her back. Sergei could taste the salt of her neck as Chekhov kissed her. He could feel her waist in the span of the man's hands. She was not beautiful. She did not look like an actress. Chekhov was thin and slightly stooped. His beard was turning grey and, at the back of his head, he was balding. The pebbles on the beach glowed white. A pair of cranes landed on the beach and stood, unreadable as hieroglyphs. When Olga pressed Chekhov's hand to her breast, Sergei felt, too, the warmth of her lover's palm against her goose-pimpled skin. The air was scented with cypresses. Nothing was stray in the last light of day, not even Sergei, unknown behind his lonely outcrop of rock, unknown to the facts, unknown to any record of the day, year or ebbing century. And when Chekhov doubled over in Olga's arms, racked with coughing, Sergei felt too the shock of it: of the wide world telescoping into a blot of blood on the white beach.

The Death of Anton Chekhov
by Anton Chekhov

Omniscience is, admittedly, a dubious gift.

Olga and I look very small indeed as we step from the carriage and peer up at the splendour of the Hotel Römerbad. Above its mansard roof and towers, the swallows dip and soar, and like them, I can see the balding crown of my own head and the soft yellow flutter of a handkerchief as Olga pats the heat from my face. It is humid, and the trees of the estate stoop under lush canopies of every shade of green. 'This weather needs to break,' Olga tells me. But I'm distracted by a swallow as it swoops low to drink from the hotel's ornamental pond; it neither pauses in its flight nor misses a single wingbeat.

Coins glint in Olga's palm as she tips our driver. I watch a porter manhandle our bags. Thank God he does. It is work enough to find my hat and straighten my bow-tie, not to mention myself, for I am bent and irritable after the long journey.

On the train from Moscow, in our stifling compartment, and likewise from Berlin, I hardly slept. But by day, I nodded off and dreamed at times of the Steppe, of my brother Alexander and I awake under the watchful stars, in grass that was as tall and alive as we were.

But Olga and my physician agree a German spa is what I need, not the wilderness of the Steppe – and I suppose I am no longer fit for sleeping in gullies or in the lee of ancient burial mounds.

When I was fifteen, my brother and I spent one last summer there, lodging with the family of a long-standing tenant of my father's. They were Cossacks and owned a ranch, and were as wild and uncouth as my family were pious and fearful. The floor was earthen, the roof was made of straw, their goat shared the rug on which we slept and the walls of the house were covered in sabres, pistols and whips. Every Sunday, the old Cossack grandmother made goose soup that tasted of greasy bathwater, and she told tales around the turf fire. Each began in the same way: 'There was a time and no time.'

As Olga and I arrive at the hotel, it is both 17th June and 30 June. The Julian calendar of Russia disagrees with the Gregorian calendar of Europe. Thirteen days slip like loose kopeks into the coat lining of the universe, and as we follow our porter through the wide doors, I suspect that we, like my Cossack crone, have been drawn into a cosmic secret: *There is a time and no time.*

At the front desk, the Maître d'Hôtel regards us over the rims of his pince-nez. His face is a pickled onion. It's clear that my personage offends him. I am far too thin and look like I haven't slept – largely because I haven't. I'm aware I smell of medication and illness. I am bad-tempered because I haven't seen a single well-dressed woman from Berlin to Badenweiler, nor one who was not trimmed with some kind of absurd braid. The Maître d'Hôtel eyes the little spittoon that pokes from my jacket pocket.

You're bad for business, his eyes say. *We are a health spa, not a sanatorium.*

I smell the faint mineral stink of the baths. At the height of the season, the village of Badenweiler's population of 700 swells to nearly 7,000.

Olga believes the Maître d'Hôtel pockets the daily visitor's tax.

The peace, quiet and order of Germany unnerve me. Scarcely a dog barks here. It would be easy to feel dead already were it not for the sound of the band rising above the Kurpark. No version of any afterlife could feature an oompah band.

As we sign the hotel register, I am already plotting my escape. We will go to Norway. My next play will be set on an ice-bound ship. We will see the Arctic Circle. What could be more thrilling than white vistas of ice and endless horizonless views?

Our room is pristine – all gleaming furniture and white linen. Olga, I see, has packed a bedpan. She is a marvel.

She bounces on each bed and takes the one by the window.

At the writing desk, I compose a hasty note to my mother:

The bread in Germany is wonderful. I eat butter, enormous quantities. The coffee is excellent. There is no decent tea. (We have brought our own.) I am already better. My legs no longer ache, and I walk about much of the day. My asthma is nearly gone, I have no diarrhoea and I am beginning to get fat. Yours, Anton.

Two days later, after a carriage ride into the mountains and a feast of a dinner, some of which I even managed to eat, the Maître d'Hôtel approaches our table and explains something to Olga in German in a terse, low voice. We have not yet had our coffee and strudel, but she pushes back her chair, and I can but trail after. In our room, she kicks her valise, still open on the floor, and tears come into her eyes.

'What is it, dear heart?' I ask. 'Whatever it is, it's nothing to us. That man is nothing to us.'

'We have to leave,' she says.

'Yes, let's leave. The restaurant is second-rate. The tea is like spittle. The bar is a morgue. We'll plan a new itinerary – Norway it is! – and leave at the end of the week.'

'Tomorrow,' she says. 'We have to leave tomorrow morning. He claims your coughing disturbs the other guests.'

The palpitations start up in my chest. 'Excellent. You know how restless I get.' I press her to me. 'Whatever happens, dearest Olya, don't get upset. Everything they say is for the best. Absolutely everything.'

On both 20th June and 3rd July we depart the Hotel Römerbad for a perfectly decent lodging house on the other side of the Kurpark.

'No balcony,' Olga laments.

'No stairs!' I sing.

In the mornings, Olga finds me the Russian papers, and translates the German ones. In the afternoon, I play patience, and she narrates the daily dramas that unfold outside the Badenweiler post office. I tell her that Germany is incapable of drama. Everyone is far too well-behaved. But she assures me that a man is hurriedly posting a letter, that a dog truly does lift its leg against a lamp post and that a child falls down and scrapes its knee. I tell her the tedium of Badenweiler will kill me even if the TB does not.

How I long for the dirt and commotion of Moscow.

Later, we sit in the park until the sun goes down. Then, in our room, Olga injects me with morphia and rubs my feet. Sometimes I sleep.

My next terrible coughing fit is, it turns out, a godsend, for it introduces us to Dr Schwoerer, the only interesting man ever to have resided in Badenweiler. He is a sunburnt, handsome sort, and his face bears the scars of youthful duels. He bear-hunts every other year in Russia, and his laughter is a distraction from the fearful oompah of my heart.

He arranges a comfortable balcony room for us at the Hotel Sommer, where he is doctor-in-residence. On 24th June and 7th July we install ourselves. His Russian wife delivers a samovar to our room. Olga beams. 'Decent tea at last!'

Which is just as well. Dr Schwoerer forbids me coffee. My heart can't take it, he says. It's working double-time as a result of my lungs' dereliction of duty. I ask him if that is the reason for the dearth of well-turned-out women in Germany. 'Exactly!' he booms. 'Your heart must have no excuse to stop. Every dreadful dirndl is just for you!'

His regimen is strict. At 7.00, I am brought tea in bed. I must stay in bed and not wander. At half seven, a masseur appears and rubs me down with warm water. I must lie still until eight, when Olga helps me to dress, and acorn cocoa is brought to our room, with bread and an immense quantity of butter. Then I am permitted fresh air in the park until lunchtime. Later,

I scribble ideas in my notebook, or sit and chat with Lev Rabenek, who reads me the latest news of Russia's doomed war with Japan.

Lev is a University of Moscow student. He has a long, pensive face and a humble, nuanced intelligence. He is in Badenweiler while his brother overcomes a melancholy – which descended as they ascended a Swiss alp.

My bird's-eye view widens. I see that, in the years to come, Lev will struggle to embrace the Revolution and will leave for London. He will pass his youth and middle years in the leafy borough of South Kensington, where he will sometimes loiter in a red-brick museum, staring, bewildered, at the catalogued jewels of the Tsarina, or the toy of an Imperial child, or the stage notes of Stanislavsky, who was a friend of his family's.

I am so easy in Lev's company that I sometimes drift off and return to the Steppe, to its vast ocean of land, to the hymn of the lark, the cry of the kite and the mystery of the kurgans – those earthen mounds which tower over everything on the endless plain.

I see the river where the Cossack girls bathed while Alexander and I spied on their nakedness from the gully. I see the ancient well, and beside it, the beautiful, fierce-eyed girl who let me kiss her, and kissed me back, as we stood for solemn, dizzying minutes without speaking a word.

In the night, Olga eases herself gently into my bed, lays my head on her breast and will not allow me to forget that I am still alive.

We sleep under only a sheet, for a heatwave has come and there is no relief. By day in the park, even my light woollen suit is unbearable, so Olga travels to Freiburg to have two flannel suits made up: one, white with a blue stripe; the other, light blue with a white stripe.

It is in the small hours of both 2nd July and 15th July that my heart stops. Lev is with us, and the good doctor too, whom Lev roused from his bed. I hear Olga gasp. I see her grab our friend the doctor by the lapels and insist he *do* something. But dead or alive, my heart is stubborn, and no amount of crushed ice will persuade it to start. Dr Schwoerer shakes his head, and I feel Lev tenderly close my eyes.

Lev leads Olga to our balcony and speaks with her until dawn. As the sky pales, they smell the hay from the fields. Somewhere a bell ringer practises. Later that day, Lev and Dr Schwoerer have a job getting me into the white-and-blue suit for my laying out. I never was anyone's straight man, and true to myself, I died doubled up on my side.

Never let it be said that I don't amuse myself.

I am reliably informed that the authorities would much prefer it if I *didn't* amuse myself, for, as I narrate the story of my own demise, it would seem I fall foul of Decree No. 02030, issued by the Central Office. This thoughtful decree bans 'the publication of any letter or book that might trivialise or discredit Anton Chekhov'.

On my head, be it.

In the corridor outside our room, the doctor and the Maître d'Hôtel are arguing. Finally I am removed from the hotel under the cover of darkness in – how fantastic! – a hotel laundry basket. At 6'1", there is nothing for it: this corpse can only sit up.

Olga and a small procession of acquaintances bear me to a nearby chapel. The light from two lanterns plays upon my face, and I seem to wear a most inappropriate smile.

You couldn't make it up.

Of course travel arrangements for the dead rarely achieve the *gravitas* of the grave. In the end, the Russian Embassy commandeers a train – or, to be specific, a refrigerated car marked 'Oysters'.

I never subscribed to any heroic ideal.

I am happy to be mistaken for an oyster.

Before my departure, Olga and the embassy staff try their reverent best to sing the *panikhida* from the train platform, but, true to form, the German authorities approach and ask them to be quiet.

Hear, hear, I say.

I am met at the station in Petersburg by the Temporary President of Russia's Literary Foundation. When Olga asks where the *Permanent* President is, she is informed that the poor man is down with the human variety of foot-and-mouth disease.

I am transferred to a red luggage car and hurtle onward to my beloved Moscow. Just as I was happy to be taken for an oyster, I am now content to be mistaken for baggage. It's true I would be a poor first-class steamer trunk, but I believe I have the makings of an excellent carpet bag.

The Berlin correspondent of the *Russian Gazette,* a fine chap called Dmitri with whom I chatted often at the hotel, tearfully cables the news of my death to Moscow, France and even London. In Britain, *The Times Literary Supplement* will conclude: 'He may or may not have been a man of genius.'

No one can equivocate as unequivocally as the English.

I bow down before them.

Myself, I give my stories six years until they are forgotten — seven at best.

It is in the darkness of the railway car that the Cossack girl appears. She leads me through the columns of luggage and over the gleaming railway tracks into the warmth of the day. We pass Moscow's golden domes, and are suddenly and strangely at the Steppe. The grass is chest high. Butterflies flash in the milkwort. I see our well, and beyond it, the low entrance to the kurgan. When I hesitate, she tugs on my hand.

Inside, it is airy and unexpectedly dry. I haven't breathed so freely in years. The walls are lined in white stone.

At my feet, I see the debris of my life: the birch rod my father used ruthlessly upon us; my stethoscope, spectacles and pocket telescope; my accursed spittoon; my fox-fur greatcoat; the landscapes painted by dear Levitan, gone before me; the proofs of *The Cherry Orchard*, which I corrected only a month ago on a Sunday in Moscow as its 250 church bells rang out.

Deep in the mound, I see the bones of nomad chiefs and wandering mystics. I long for Olga, for her bright eyes and cool hand. I am heartsick, too, for Alexander, for my sister Masha and my mother; for the sun through the willow tree by the house in Yalta; for the dolphins leaping in the Bay; for a sleigh ride over fresh snowfall on Moscow streets.

'I am afraid,' I say to the Cossack girl.

But it's too late. *There is a time and no time*. Before I can stop her hand, she heaves open a door at the back of the kurgan. There is a surge of light and heat, a great thermal uplift, a tugged loop of time and being — and, before I can take possession of myself, I am looking down once more on Olga outside the Hotel Römerbad as she tips our driver. The coins glint in her hand. Thirteen days rush back upon themselves in a collision of cloud, shadow, heat and electricity. 'This weather needs to break,' Olga tells me. I see the porter usher us in. We have just arrived. I swoop to the pond, drink, then rise, tail streamers dripping. I see my old self linger for a moment more. Hand to his eyes, he follows my flight, eyes squinting, as I strain towards Norway and the Pole.

How to Make a Citizen's Arrest

Ensure there is no possibility of a police officer doing the job for you.

In the night of Harrowby Street, we're alone. You stoop into the wind to peer, your expression strained but benign. It wasn't easy to catch you up – you have a long stride. Behind us, in Edgware Road, we hear a police siren go up like a war cry.

Try to stay calm.

I squeeze your hand but I do not let go. Your fingers, I notice, are cold against mine. In your other hand, you clasp a carrier bag, and through the transparent polythene, I see a beef fettucini meal-for-one. Your coat flaps in the wind. Your knuckles are white. I'd imagined you to be the sort of man who wore good gloves on nights like this.

London seems abandoned. Only a few pass. They study their phones as they walk, each face sombre and ghoulishly uplit. Around us, the night seems to stretch and thicken, and my phone vibrates endlessly with the news alerts.

'No,' I explain to you over the buzzing, 'no, I don't want a selfie – but thank you.' Will it help to clarify? 'I'm not wired either,' I say.

'"Weird?"' You cup your free hand to your ear. The wind snatches at our words.

Should I walk away now?

I see the wheels of risk assessment spinning behind your eyes. A stranger has taken hold of your hand. Is she mad? Will she scream if you forcibly separate yourself? Will she make false claims? Are we on CCTV?

You simply wanted an easy meal and an early night.

Neither of us could have dreamed it would come to this.

'It's a horrid evening,' you say, straightening. Above the bridge of your nose, the frown lines deepen. You stare at the sight of your hand locked in mine. You do not pull away, though you could do so, as we're both aware. My grip is stubborn rather than strong, and it wouldn't take a great deal of effort to overpower me. You can't, however, risk a scene. Twitter. Instagram. You have your Foundation to think of. Your face-for-hire.

It's irrelevant of course, but I don't think your ears are as large as people used to say.

'How can I help?' Your words are terse, perfunctory. You're losing patience.

I quite understand.

'If I'm honest,' I begin, 'I'm not sure you can help.' Because – how to say it? – everything is already too late.

I can feel your pulse racing in your thumb. Please bear in mind that I have no contingency for fight-or-flight. I have simply relied upon your conciliatory nature and your well-known fear of giving offence. No wonder you can't make sense – not really – of the endless public anger. After all, you're famously *nice*.

I change the subject. I tell you that today is my niece's ninth birthday. I explain that she rang me early this morning, her time, worried that Friday the 13th made her birthday unlucky. I could almost feel her sleepy warmth. 'How on earth could today be unlucky?' I asked her. 'It's the anniversary of the day we got you.' Four thousand miles away, in her wordlessness, I heard her relief. 'Do you want to speak to my mom?' she asked. Then she dropped the phone and disappeared in a happy tattoo of footsteps.

I tell you this because it reminds me that life – the running, reckless love of it – is never undone. Not by grievous errors of the past. Not by acts of deception. Not even by nights like tonight. I tell you because it is a small article of faith, and perhaps the only one that will remain to you.

Avoid acting alone.

The latest BBC alert arrives, and I have to stretch the text with my fingers so you can read it without your specs. It tells us that, in the weeks and months to come, there will be armed SAS in plain clothes on the streets of London.

But not yet, not tonight, and contrary to the best advice, it is better that we are alone; that I present no overt physical threat; that I can be honest when I tell you there is no one waiting behind any corner. I hadn't planned to see you in the Waitrose in Edgware Road. I was only after a bar of Fair Trade dark chocolate, 85% cocoa, select outlets only. I ask you: what were the chances?

You drop the carrier bag and reach into your coat pocket for what I imagine must be a closed-circuit alarm on a fob. When the fob doesn't appear, you turn your trouser pockets inside out with your one free hand. It's not easily done.

For the first time, your expression of strained tolerance fails, and I see you assess me properly. I am of average height. I am middle-aged. I wear a good mac and earrings that glimmer in the sodium light. You see it is unlikely I will catch you in a headlock or wrestle you to the ground. I do not carry an umbrella I can turn upon you. My coat pockets don't bulge with any hidden can of Mace. I can see you believe me when I say I didn't set out to follow you; that it simply seemed wrong to turn away.

The last thing you want is a scene.

I realise of course that you are comforted by the knowledge of the specialist protection unit parked outside your home in Connaught Square, only a few minutes from here. They will come looking for you. That's what you explain. Before setting off, you leaned your head through a tinted window and said you were only popping out for a ready meal. The lead officer tried to dissuade you, but you summoned your famous grin and slapped the bonnet of the vehicle.

You'd like to give me the chance to reconsider my actions.

I suppose that's something like an official pardon. It must be difficult to remember it's a power you no longer have. It must be difficult to remember a great deal.

The wind is sharp. You try to button your coat, an optimistic manoeuvre in our present circumstances. But try you do, and a boarding pass slips from your pocket. We bend simultaneously. I hear your knees crack – too many games of squash over the years.

I wish I didn't remember this kind of trivia. How strange it must be to leave miscellaneous traces in countless memories. *Do you ever pick up the guitar these days?* I want to ask. I read once that you used to do a good Mick Jagger impression, though, frankly, it's hard to imagine.

I'm good at imagining, by the way.

You retrieve your shopping and on we walk. You explain you arrived home this evening after a stopover in Dubai. Everyone was out or away (or estranged, I silently add). In spite of your housekeeper's best efforts, there was nothing you fancied in the fridge.

You're telling me, in your own uneasy way, that it was an entirely ordinary evening until I approached. You were simply another citizen with a need for comfort eating. Pasta. Carbs. It's allowed, isn't it?

'You wanted fresh air,' I say, nodding. 'Or you did once you heard the sound of gunfire.'

You turn to me, startled by my uncanny grasp, not only of your hand, but of such privacies.

Your pulse is racing again but I continue. 'The gunfire from rue Bichat – streaming through your open laptop in your kitchen.'

Writers. Sorry. We know more than we decently should.

'Before tonight,' I continue, 'it was hard enough for you. I get that. Sometimes, when you're alone at home, you see faces at the windows. They're cast in soupy green, as if they're coming to you through night-vision scopes.'

You stop short, and – given my grip – I have no choice but to do the same. But I don't spare you the details. 'When you saw them again, you hit every switch you could. You lit up the kitchen like an oper-ating theatre. You had to close your eyes and count to four as you breathed in and six as you breathed out. You had to remind yourself that the faces are only a trick your mind plays; that it rarely lasts for long. You felt hot, sweaty. You grabbed your overcoat and paused only to speak with Security outside.'

As I narrate these things – my prerogative, I'm afraid – your eyes widen and fill.

I pass you a tissue from the Boots mini-pack in my pocket.

'It's only the wind,' you claim as you dab at your face. Suddenly you look oddly vulnerable in the night. Old. 'The wind,' you repeat, 'and the long flight.' Your hair is silvered and sparse. Your face is drawn. Your eyes seem too small. Something flickers across them – guilt or shame – and then it's extinguished. Whatever happened to 'Bambi' and his bright eyes?

You clear your throat and compose your public voice. 'Listen. You seem like a perfectly nice woman. I assure you, there's no need for any awkwardness. You've simply made a mistake. Let's walk back to my house, and I'll arrange for one of my detail to give you a lift home. No harm done.'

Which is where I have to disagree.

In a city square up ahead, someone lets off a firework and, in the white flash, I see the tendons rise on your neck.

Conduct the arrest carefully, respectfully, and with, at most, a reasonable and proportionate use of force.

Naturally, you're lost for words as I tie my right hand to your left with the navy-blue fabric belt of my mac. It's absurd – I know it is – but the act of holding on tightly is bringing on my RSI.

For some reason, the sight of me winding and tying our wrists together, palm to palm, brings to mind – yes, for us both – the image of a bride and groom as their hands are bound by the priest with his stole. As you wait, I thank you for your patience. I thank you for not running away in the brief interlude in which you might have tried. Of course you fully believe I would give chase. You know your knees are bad. Best, you decide, to go quietly, until a better plan presents itself.

I stow our hands in your coat pocket. More room in there than in mine. You're embarrassed, I'm embarrassed, but we do our best to ignore our new, enforced intimacy.

Up ahead, a caff is still open. I nod to the misty window. The night weighs heavily, the line of your shoulders drops, and against my every expectation, you dip your head and follow.

After the murk of November in Harrowby Street, the light inside is yellow, so yellow it seems almost viscous. Your hand sweats in mine, as if I've led you into an interrogation room, not a Turkish café. The place is deserted apart from one old man, his cough and a gym-pumped waiter who is thumbing his phone screen. Like everyone else tonight, the waiter bows his head before the blurred-out bodies of the bewildered dead. In the foreground of our TV and phone screens, they lie where they fell.

How can it be? Only hours ago, these bodies were people who argued, laughed, yearned, looked up at the moon, worried about rent, scooped children into their arms, sipped coffee, hailed taxis and embraced. They argue with us now, rapping at the glass of cafés like this one. They have names, they say. They have homes where books lie open, where beds dip to their shape and clothes carry their scent.

Yes. I see them too.

So does the old man. That's why he turns away from the glass, pops a pinch of snuff into his mouth and shuts his eyes tight.

We stare at an empty booth. 'No place cards,' I joke. 'Do you think it's boy-girl-boy-girl?'

You turn, your expression pained.

You need to understand: there is no protocol. No modus operandi. No clear-cut way forward.

We slip into the booth, side by side. The knot at our wrists prevents any other arrangement. Direct eye contact is of course difficult.

The waiter arrives.

'Two espressos,' I say without consulting.

You stare ahead, glassy-eyed. You need a shave. Your breath is faintly stale. You still clasp your carrier bag with the unrequited fettucini. Our shoulders touch, and we sit without speaking, like unhappy teenagers in love.

Inform the subject of what is being done as soon as is reasonably possible, explaining the reason for arrest, and what offence it is you believe he/she has committed.

It's not as easy as I thought, coming out with it.

I'd like to think you're someone who can read between the lines. I'd like to spare you the familiar shock of the words.

So allow me to digress.

'I followed you once before on a September evening in '95, when you were on your way to victory. 1995. Think of it. Isis was still an Egyptian goddess. "Terror" was something I'd once studied in French History. I

remember my sister applying for a job that had something to do with what she called the "Information Super
Highway". I thought it sounded dull, a non-starter. We
were living in innocent times.

'My then-husband and I had been to the same perform-
ance as you and Cherie at the Aldwych Theatre: Tom
Stoppard's *Indian Ink*. It wasn't Stoppard at his best – as
you might recall – but, for the first time, the play didn't
matter. You and Cherie were only a few rows ahead.
The country was basking in your glow. London was
lush with what seemed an endless summer. H. and I
were fresh-faced with young love.

'You won't remember, but during the interval, in the
tiny upstairs bar, as H. queued for drinks, I spotted you.
Or rather, everyone spotted you. How could we not?

'I can still see Cherie . . . She was sheltering with
friends in a corner near the bar. She had on a pale-gold
lamé jumpsuit with a halter-neck. Her hair was a dark
confection, her lips were very red and she was laughing over her G&T. You were out for the evening with
another couple. Everyone must have wanted to be your
friend that summer.

'You stood with your party but also apart, your body
angled towards the room, as if you were its presiding
spirit. You were taller than you appeared on our small
telly at home. Your eyes were bright blue, not brown as
I'd thought. Your jacket was unbuttoned, and I noticed
you had a slight paunch. It made you look worldly
somehow. Until that night, I'd thought you to be one
of those eternally boyish, weedy sorts. I remember you
smiled warmly at the recognition in my eyes, happy
to confer upon me your gaze; happy to enjoy a long,
smoky-eyed moment of flirtation.

'I confess. I was, fleetingly, proud. When I told H., even he was proud. We were young. You and Cherie were almost young. England, you said, would be young again. It would have "soul". I remember you weren't afraid of the word. Through my telly screen, you told me, "I have complete confidence in the beliefs I hold dear."

'Well, that was no lie.

'After the Stoppard, H. and I loitered by the lobby doors, like giddy younger siblings. We followed you the distance of three streets to the steps of your private club. I can still see you, Cherie and Co. walking along the pavement in a wide row of four, as if London was yours that night. You had only to appear on the steps of the unmarked club for the door to open from the inside. We never saw the doorman. We never saw the hand.

'That night seemed perfect, as light and golden as Cherie's jumpsuit.'

An indictable offence is one that can be tried in a crown court, in front of a jury.

The waiter slaps the bill on the table, though we've hardly touched our coffees. He wants to close up, and he makes no secret of it.

You ask if I would do you the favour of getting to the point. Talk of your early years as Leader – of all that hope – seems to have hit a nerve. Though tempted, I don't turn to observe the discomfort on your face. I look straight ahead, for you are entitled to a degree of privacy. Even here, in a cheap leatherette booth, in the glaring light of a backstreet caff, I want to ensure you have that.

I too find it difficult: the loss of so much hope; the knowledge that something too big for me to name or describe – a new, dread reality that bounces off satellites and travels in hair-thin fibres beneath ocean floors – has overcome our ability even to imagine it.

You were meant to be a checkpoint. Instead, you waved it through – whatever 'it' finally turns out to be. You opened the gates with a lie.

You're quite right. Writers lie. Yes. We do.

I begin again. I say: 'We all have blind spots. You wanted to be decent. I understand that. You wanted to be loyal. Sometimes, it's hard not to be a people-pleaser. I err that way myself. And who *would* want to risk a Special (capital S) Relationship (capital R) at a time like that? Who, under such desperate circumstances, *would* want to look like a person – a statesman – who was prepared to cut and run?

'Far easier – when it came to it – to overlook the dubiousness of the Intelligence; to trust Intelligence to be – yes, I'm with you – *intelligent.*'

I pause. 'I'm trying to imagine your thinking. Did the British public *actually* need to know that North Korea, in all likelihood, possessed a greater stockpile than Iraq? No, they did not. You took an executive decision. Someone had to. Hindsight is a beautiful thing, but could *anyone* have predicted a war that would never end? Could anyone have foreseen such—'

'Chaos.' You finish my sentence. I look up. Your face looks clammy; your eyes, depthless.

At the till, our waiter is still staring, slack-jawed, at Paris on his phone screen.

'It's warm,' you say. 'May I take off my coat?'

I shake my head. 'He wants to close up.' I drop a fiver on the table, and the waiter stares as we sidle out of the booth, a pair of urban oddities. He's too young to recognise you, and you have no choice but to retract the famous-person smile you were about to offer.

In the event that you do act alone, be aware it is your word against theirs.

Our footsteps echo too loudly in Seymour Place. My phone is ringing in my pocket. I check – it's Evie, my niece, on Facetime – and swipe the Decline button, though I immediately feel the loss of her there in the windswept street.

I draw breath. It is important to marshal the facts. 'You had firm information, or you said you did. You had shockingly clear intelligence. Forty-five minutes to take cover. Yet MI6 admitted to the UN's Mexican Ambassador that the evidence was neither clear nor firm. With respect, if MI6 found themselves able to update the Mexican Ambassador, would they not have seen fit to tell you? And in the meantime, on the Arabian Peninsula, the troops were battle-ready.'

You stop on the pavement. 'Define "battle-ready".'

I sigh and tug you on.

Our hands are stowed once more in your coat pocket. My own still buzzes with BBC alerts. Now and then, you flinch, as if one of them has given you an electric shock. The elegant Georgian homes of Seymour Place flicker with the night's news. Through the thin panes, we hear the shots ring out again and again.

I continue. I try to speak plainly. 'That spring, Lord G. couldn't make the legal case – and then, lo, he could.'

We turn into George Street. You remind me that your Security team are out looking for you. You close your eyes in a display of polite weariness. 'Any professional person is entitled to change his view.'

'Especially after a trip to Washington?'

You roll your eyes. The mood between us has shifted. You are over the shock of my appearance in your evening. You won't dignify my question with an answer. After so many years, it's banal to your ears.

Even so, I press on. 'Whether Lord G. endorsed or didn't endorse, what does it matter? One can't "disappear" the truth.'

You smile, humouring me. 'Which in your view is?'

I repeat the obvious. 'No UN Resolution. Which in turn meant' – I might have added jazz-hands were I not one hand down – 'you blamed Chirac. Played the anti-French card. Created a distraction. Then seized the moral high ground, and did what you were going to do all along.'

At the crossing, a car stops for us. You nod your thanks to the driver.

For years, you've hidden in plain view.

A civilian may conduct an arrest if a breach of the peace is or was committed in his/her presence.

Who was *not* present? The action, after all, was dubbed 'Shock and Awe'.

That first night, thirty-six Tomahawk cruise missiles exploded over Baghdad. Each released its own arsenal of cluster bombs. Each cluster exploded into 'submunitions'. It rained fire.

On my television screen, Baghdad, a city I had known only through *The Arabian Nights*, lost every mystery. It seemed impossible that a sole palm tree in the foreground could stand untouched by the apocalypse.

Perhaps you understand why I couldn't simply walk away with my bar of chocolate. I smiled at you in that theatre bar. I voted. I cheered.

The civilian may conduct an arrest if he/she has reasonable grounds to believe that such an arrest is necessary to prevent the person being arrested from making off before a constable can assume responsibility for him.

I didn't mean to blurt it out. I meant to remain detached.

'You've made off so often and so well that people get the door for you on your way out. But tonight – be honest – you don't want to go home. You would have shaken me off by now if you did. After all, who else but me knows about the panic attacks in the night? You need – you badly want – someone to understand it's exhausting to be you. Denial is draining. You know that better than anyone. But what, you ask yourself over and over, is the alternative? Can anyone ever tell you that?'

Your eyebrows mimic confusion. You bluff well. This, too, I understand. There are things you cannot bear to utter; thoughts you can only dedicate silently to the night air and the hallowed ministrations of November.

St James's Church rises over us in its stony repose. Tonight, its door is wide open and bears a simple handwritten sign: 'For those wishing to pray for Paris'. Inside, we see three or four darkened shapes kneeling in pews, their shoulders hunched and their heads bowed. We gaze up at the dizzying, vaulted space. At the candle rack, I force a twenty-pound note through the coin slot. 'For all the faces at the windows?' I say.

You don't meet my eyes but you take the taper I offer. Together, we light every votive candle and stub on the rack, and as the flames swell into a blaze, I check Google on my phone. The nearest station is just a mile away. Paddington Green.

Any video or sound recording of what led you to act may be helpful when it comes to explaining to the police why you have stepped into the breach.

Your knees crack again as we genuflect and take a pew near the rear of the church. The belt at our wrists chafes. Your stomach rumbles. Your carrier bag is leaking defrosted beef. I reach for my bar of chocolate and extend it to you. The gold wrapping flashes as we open it together, one hand each, in a paltry rendition of Hopkins's 'shook foil'. (You know the reference. You enjoyed poetry at school.)

We work awkwardly as a team to snap off jagged corners, then eat without speaking. The pew is cold and hard. When I huff, I can see my breath. Everything smells of candle wax, dust and incense.

We slide towards one another, for warmth. For a time, we nod off, my head against your shoulder; your chin on your chest.

When we awake, we are alone in the church and my phone is alive again, its ringtone echoing off every saint and martyr. I blindly thumb it, and from 4,000 miles away, Evie's face grins up at me, her lips stained red with party drink. 'Hi,' she says. Then she blows hard on a party horn.

It squeals.

She looks pleased with herself. 'Did it pop out in England?'

I raise a finger to my lips. 'Not quite. I'm in church. Did you have a fun birthday?'

'Uh-huh.'

'Any nice prezzies?'

She points her iPad lens. I turn up the light on my display. A shiny new music keyboard with a gigantic blue bow comes into view.

'Oh!' I exclaim. '*Fancy*.'

You lean in to see and grin. I dimly remember: you're a father of four. You've been a devoted parent. You loved it all, especially when they were small. You miss it now. The house seems cavernous. Even the youngest must be almost grown.

No wonder you brood on your legacy. He was only – what? – three when you invaded Iraq. Now you need him, above all, to know there was a world before; that you were someone else – someone different; that you haven't only made the world a more dangerous place.

Evie reappears. 'Is he your new boyfriend?'

I smile. 'No.'

'Oh.' She sticks the blue bow to the side of her head and runs, clutching her iPad, past walls dotted with balloons. 'Wait there!'

'Wait for what?' I call to her ceiling.

She lines up the camera's lens and crosses to her new keyboard. She wears a white turtleneck, blue-and-white horizontal striped leggings, and now, the blue bow. Her back is slim. Her blonde head shines in the nimbus of a lamp. Individual hairs rise from her head; she has been rubbing balloons against it for much of the day. Through the window beside her, daylight still illumines her world and, as she flips unceremoniously through the pages of a music book, we watch fat flakes of snow falling softly over the Gatineau River. Through lenses and windowpanes, I can just make out white frozen swathes of river and the darker melt-holes of November.

On the candle rack near the altar, the flames tremble and flare, and the darkness of the church flexes. Then she jiggles her shoulders, shakes her hand and with three small fingers, punches the keys.

'Ode to Joy' rises haltingly into the vastness above us.

You tilt your head back. I bow mine. The simple melody washes over us as if it is composed of chords of light. It moves through Evie's small, knuckle-less hands to flood every crack and crevice in the church; every font, chalice and angel's O of a mouth. It rings from every flagstone.

Her face reappears at the screen. 'That's all I know.'

'I loved it,' I say. 'I *really* loved it.'

'Me too,' you say. Your voice is raw.

Later, when I am asked why I followed you tonight, I will resist the urge to speak of her, of who and what we leave behind.

Evie picks up the party horn again and blows till it pokes out, sharp and hard as a tongue.

'Did it pop into England that time?' she asks.

I shake my head. 'Blow harder.'

'No,' she sighs. 'That not what I need to do.' She huffs her fringe out of her eyes and presses her fingertips to what, on my screen, looks like its bright underside.

You lean in as the coin of darkness appears in the bright display. Together we watch it slowly, slowly widen and spread until it covers the place where Evie's mouth should be. We see her dimpled hands reposition her hair bow on the side of her head, but her mouth and chin are gone. Within moments, her entire face is lost from view, but the horn squeals again, and this time its pink-and-blue tip darts into the darkness of the church. We flinch as it coils back into her world.

'Did it reach that time?' she calls.

'Yes,' I say through the trance of the moment. 'Yes, it did.'

She fingers the screen again, plying the small patch of on-screen darkness, as if she is working a piece of black plasticine, stretching it ever outward. I watch her white turtleneck disappear beneath it. 'Evie,' I say. 'Stop doing that. 'Stop. I can't see you.' The back of my neck has gone cold.

Beside me, you squeeze my hand, and I am grateful.

She is a blur of pink fingertips, pushing and swiping.

'Evie!' I call sternly.

'Wait!' she bosses.

The puddle of darkness becomes a rectangle. The rectangle outgrows the dimensions of my screen and phone. The light from the candle rack swells, the nave is illumined, our pew gleams suddenly and, as we stare, a melt-hole opens up in the dark air before us.

A party horn falls between our feet. I hear you inhale sharply. A snowflake lands on my cheek. Then a blue bow flutters into the footwell, and Evie drops, red-cheeked and breathing hard.

'Since when can you do that?' I say.

She shrugs, picks up the party horn and sticks the bow back on her head. 'I figured it out.'

She smells of fresh winter air and Tide detergent.

'I wanted to see your boyfriend.'

'He's not my boyfriend.'

'Did he like my song?'

Your eyes are bright for the first time tonight. Somehow, Evie, the force of her, has returned you, us, from the gloom into life.

'I thought it was very' – you stutter with a humility that is not feigned – 'beautiful. It must have been hard to learn in just one day.'

'"Joy" is easy actually. For me it is, I mean.' She frowns. 'But not for everyone.'

'I appreciate that. What I meant was—'

She puts her finger to her lips and looks up high to the unseeable. She hears it before we do. Overhead, a helicopter has found its coordinates over the church tower. Her spell is broken.

'*At last,*' you breathe. 'May I?' You snatch my phone. Evie climbs into my lap and plugs her ears against a thrum of blades and propellers that grows louder and louder. You sign into Twitter one-handed. It doesn't take you long to show me the shot of us walking in Seymour Street. You find another shot, dark and grainy, of the two of us asleep in the pew; you show me, as if to say, it was always going to end like this. Didn't you try to tell me?

'I don't want you to worry unduly,' you say. 'They'll have to question you. It won't be altogether pleasant. But I give you my word: I won't press charges. And I'll ask someone to make appropriate arrangements for your niece.'

Evie locks her arms around my neck. 'I don't like him, Aunt Ali. Why did you let him hear "Joy"?'

I lower her to the floor and help her straighten her stripy leggings. Then we rise from the pew as three and turn. From the dense shadow of the church's porch, the broad shapes of two policemen materialise.

Before I have time to explain, Evie drops to the floor and covers her head with her arms.

I crouch down beside her, quickly, to reassure, and, beside me, still tied to me, you stagger.

'Suicide bombers,' she whispers. 'Get down, Aunt Ali! Play dead.'

'No, I promise, sweetheart. They're—'

She nods fiercely, tears in her eyes – *yes, yes* – and mimes the bulk of their vests.

'*Police,*' I mouth. 'Police . . .'

She's trembling.

Behind me, you try. 'Don't be frightened, Evie. I know these men. Now be a good girl and—'

But she won't get up. I suspect she can't.

Regardless, I feel your strength, raising me to my feet, propelling me past her, forward and down the aisle. Your hand grips mine. There is no confetti. No rice for luck. We pass under the archway and into the porch. You clear your throat and find your public voice.

This is how you begin.

'Gosh. I must say, I'm rather relieved to see you two.' You have to shout over the noise of the helicopters that hover now above the treetops. A drone zips, already collecting footage. Outside, beyond the deep chill of the porch, people gather – passers-by, your Twitter followers, stray members of the press. You cannot suppress a smile of relief.

You hold up our bound wrists. You make a comical face to your Security chaps. Your meaning is clear: *we've got a live one here.*

You say: 'I thought it best simply to wait it out till you turned up. No real harm done.' You appear magnanimous, unflustered. You draw us into the night air and breathe deeply.

One of the officers unties the belt.

'Evie?' I call over my shoulder.

But nothing.

Your Security Unit instruct me to remain where I am. I rub my wrist. 'Evie!'

Overhead, the drone's camera registers the red thermographic surge of my heart.

In the first instance, it is important to be clear and concise.

The shorter of the two officers asks my name and notes my address. I wait for him to look up from the screen where he scratches with a stylus. The radio on his belt crackles with fragments of voices. Next to it, a can of CS spray glints. The yellow pistol-shaped thing on his belt is, I hope, a taser only. I rehearse my words inwardly. Composure is important. A squad car's light spins in the darkness beyond us.

I realise that my eyes are closed and my lips are moving faintly. The man pauses in his questions to permit me to utter what he mistakes for a prayer.

I look up. I breathe from my diaphragm. (*Be advised that the government does not publish a complete list of offences.*) What are the words?

This is how I begin.

'It is my duty to report' – I see you turn slowly, your eyes huge – 'that I've arrested this man for a breach of the peace.'

Deer.

Headlights.

Bambi.

Why do I, in spite of myself, worry for you?

Somewhere behind us, on the floor, Evie is still shaking.

We Are Methodists

Toby – he tells me he's called Toby – heaves his toolbox and himself up the spiral of my staircase. Toby is a plumber. A heating engineer. I am a client. A new homeowner.

We know our parts.

At the top of the staircase, he stands and stares. Above us, the old chapel window rises twenty-five feet to a vast pine arch. Once, this window was a Methodist view on Creation, on the hills of East Brighton and its glittering sea.

'That's something,' he says, and is slow to turn away. Through the clear panes, to the north-east, the green flanks of the Downs rear up with spring. To the south, the sea is silvered in the midday light. Above the chimney pots, the gulls are ecstatic.

He counts the panes with his eyes. From floor to ceiling, eight bright stems of glass rise up, five panes high, until they burst, high overhead, into four golden arches. The arches, in turn, bloom into three circular windows. What is it about circles? I don't know. I suspect Toby doesn't know. Heads back, chins up, we're moved to silence. At the top of my staircase, suspended in a moment we will soon disregard, we're strangers.

'Coffee?' I ask.

I move into the organ loft that is now my kitchen.

He blinks. 'Thank you. Yes. Milk, one sugar.'

I dig in the boxes marked 'Kitchen Cupboards, 3 of 6'. My things seem unfamiliar. I find cups but no saucers. Toby opens the boiler cupboard and prises off the casing. He is stocky with a low belly. Early forties, I estimate. An oversized tattoo runs up his forearm through the curling dark hair: 'MADISON', it reads in cursive lettering.

It's Day One of our four-day works schedule. Toby tells me, haltingly, that, this morning, he'll do the full boiler service. The boiler is old, so he'll check the controls and clear away dirt and debris; he'll do a gas analysis to monitor carbon monoxide; he'll confirm there are no weeping joints; he'll test the circuitry, the fan pressure and the inlet pressure. He'll inspect the heat exchanger and the burner. He'll clean out the condensate trap.

Toby's mouth has seen better days. His front teeth are missing, along with the cuspids and miscellaneous others. I hear the soft nasal sing-song of a Birmingham accent. I imagine backstreet punch-ups in his youth.

He speaks quickly, mistrustful of his mouth, but finally, he nods, relieved to have got through the speech. Later I'll be sent an electronic survey from his company; it will ask me to confirm that, prior to the given job, Toby explained the full nature of it.

'Thank you.' I pass him a steaming coffee. 'You've made everything clear.'

He nods. His head is small and neat, almost feral; his hair is shorn close to his scalp. The dark stubble along his jawline is flecked with grey, and his eyelashes are thick like a child's. He lowers them often.

When his phone starts to vibrate, he sighs. 'Hi, love. Can't. On a job. I'll call you later, right?' He slides the phone into a pocket. 'My girlfriend,' he explains. 'She's a lot younger.' He smiles apologetically. 'She does my head in.'

'That's wonderful,' I hear myself say. I make no sense.

Toby reaches, quickly, for a pair of pliers.

I blush and lift the vase of nearly dead tulips from the kitchen table. At the sink, I turn away and let the water run and run. I cannot say what I actually meant: that I hope his broken mouth will kiss and be kissed. I cannot say it because what could it possibly matter to me?

In recent days, the tulips drooped, drowsy as narcoleptics. Now, their yellow heads are full-blown, too weighty for their slender stems and leaves. Since yesterday, they've been resting only millimetres above the tabletop, a lost cause. I fill the vase anyway.

Toby keeps his eyes, front and centre, on the boiler's innards. I switch on Radio 4, waiting for its calm to neutralise the atmosphere; to cover the odd sense of domesticity into which we've been cast. The proximity of strangers is a peculiar thing, and the open-plan design means there is nowhere to hide. I unpack dishes, pots, canisters, oven mitts, a stray pair of socks and bra. I stuff the latter in a kitchen drawer.

Even so, when it happens, it seems wrong not to risk it, wrong not to say, 'Look. Toby, look at the tulips.' He turns, I point and, together, we watch the oversized heads rise, infinitesimally higher and higher, in an act of blind, magnificent will.

'You wouldn't think,' he murmurs.

'No,' I breathe.

I fold tea towels and behold the resurrection. He tinkers again in the boiler cupboard, glancing back to watch it over his shoulder. Before long, the tulips are half their natural height and still rising.

'Life,' he says. 'Bloody stubborn, isn't it.'

We find our equilibrium.

'Biscuit?' I venture.

He shakes his head and adjusts a pressure valve. 'Never eat in the day.'

'No breakfast?'

'Coffee only – till dinner time.'

There's something fight-or-flight-like in his bearing, a potential clenched in his shoulders. Yet his movements are slow, wary. 'See this dial?'

I walk to his side.

'The needle should hover around the *one* mark. When it's too low, just top it up, with this black knob.'

'Right.' I nod. 'Yes.'

He picks up his coffee. We look to the sea. Half a dozen sailboats navigate the dazzle, white sails tipping on the breeze.

'That's a view,' he says.

'Yes,' I say.

At home in Portslade, if he crooks his head a certain way in his toddler's room, he can just see a skinny 'V' of sea. He has a fishing boat which he hasn't had out since his youngest – Madison – was born. It's moored at Newhaven, waiting to be scraped and sanded. He says: 'I know I should say "she", like all the marina types do, but I always feel daft saying that.'

'I do too,' I say. I fold another tea towel. 'Maybe the "she" of me resists.'

'Feminist,' he says. 'That explains it.'

I look up. 'Explains what?'

'Being good looking and on your own.' He carries on tinkering in the cupboard. 'Me, I'm ugly and *surrounded*. Ex-wife always on the blower. Our son up in Stoke getting himself into trouble. My girlfriend. Her mates in our kitchen most nights of the week. I used to wonder why they behaved like teenagers till I realised they *are* teenagers, or not far off. Then there's her mother tutting and painting her toenails on the *Radio Times*. Not to mention our three kiddies. Each night when I get home, the two older boys are either on the PlayStation or torturing the cat. Forgot to mention the cat. One old, incontinent cat.' He looks up. 'It's a madhouse basically.'

These days, he says, the boat is like someone else's memory. So he makes do with an old reel near Hove Lagoon, at the edge of Fatboy Slim's private beachfront. As he speaks, he draws his arm back and casts an imaginary line in a long fluid gesture. Suddenly he is supple. His eyes shine.

But his fishing is interrupted by his phone. 'A perfect demonstration,' he tells me, 'of why I never take my phone when I'm off out with my reel.'

I turn off the radio.

'Like I said, love – can't.' He rolls his eyes for my benefit, then stabs the phone with his finger, and returns to the gauge hooked up to the boiler.

I hold out a packet of biscuits. 'Sure?'

He waves it politely away. 'I hear my kids say, "I'm starving! Dad, I'm *starving*." As if.' He starts to laugh, then draws in his upper lip.

I carry on unpacking boxes and smile. 'We have no idea, do we?' Olive oil. Balsamic. Sea salt. Quinoa. Wild rice. Omega oil and green tea supplements.

The boiler fires up, so that, at first, I hardly hear him. 'It's an agony,' he says. 'Plain and simple.'

I straighten.

'After the first week it gets a little easier. Because your body is giving up, and your head feels like it's floating away.' His words are a fast-moving stream. 'And that's what calms you down finally, what saves you, that floating feeling, as you start to die.' He turns and stares through the window at the twenty-five feet of consecrated sky.

In the direct light, lines and shadows appear on his face. I stand, clutching vitamin bottles.

Then he walks across the room to the nearest radiator and turns the bleed key. His hands are small and solid, but the joints on his fingers look overlarge, misshapen. A silence opens up between us, wide as a crevasse. His brow tightens, then in he lurches. 'There were four of us. All from the 42nd Commando Division. We were dropped into a port town near Basra. Iraq. March 2003. You know.' He glances up, smiling faintly. 'That malarkey.'

I nod. I fold my arms. To be steady.

'One minute, you're up in the Hercules, breathing in a hundred per-cent oxygen so you don't get the bends, and the next minute you're in free fall for the longest fifteen seconds of your life. You have to pull the ripcord when you're crazy high up – twenty-five thousand feet – because otherwise, the sound of the chutes opening might be detected by the enemy lower down. The world is roaring around you and at the same time everything's deadly quiet, and the four of us form up in a stack, like quadruplets waiting to drop. All you want is to feel the ground beneath your feet. The chap at the bottom of the stack is the one with the compass. No GPS for us then. We're drifting cross-country, across a desert without landmarks, and just praying we don't freeze to death as we do. It's minus twenty-nine degrees in the air, then forty-five degrees in the Drop Zone when we hit. Nothing prepares you for that.

'The truth is, nothing prepares you for most of it. When you do land, it's all rock and sand, so everything's always giving way underfoot. You can hardly run. Not even when you're twenty-three and fitter than you'll ever be again and your life depends on it' – his voice drops – 'which it did more or less.' He shrugs. 'Got ourselves captured on Day One, didn't we.' His eyes darken and the lashes dip.

'God,' I say. 'How awful.'

The radiator bangs and chokes, as if the dust of the desert is here too. 'Air lock,' he says.

He glances up, checking that I'm okay; checking that I'm not checking the clock. Then he looks away again. 'They left us tied to metal chairs in that heat. Four of us in a row in a concrete courtyard. By the second week, they didn't even need to tie us up because there was nowhere to go. No way out and no way back inside. We were dehydrated. Starving. We sat till we fell off. You only knew you'd fallen off when you came to on the ground. After a point, you were just glad of the chair. You're baking in the heat but you love your bloody chair.'

'I'm so sorry,' I say.

'I never had much religion but what I had left me out there.'

I pull out two kitchen chairs. Neither of us sits.

'Of course,' I say. 'No wonder.'

'No wonder. No feeling. No nothing after. Because all that heat gets inside you and it flares sometimes. Like when my mates go on about their Sky being on the blink. Or when my ex-wife gets upset because I won't help pay for her European city break. Or when I see a busker in Brighton. Ever seen that chap in the zebra costume playing piano in East Street? I think, is he why we were tied to chairs? So he could dress like a zebra and play the piano? Did I join up so that, one day, my kids could feel deprived if they weren't given two-for-one Cadbury eggs? Not that I'm complaining. All that's *normal*. It's *not* normal to prefer fish to people. I know that. It's *not* normal to get worked up about a grown man who calls himself Fatboy Slim and owns the best of the flipping beachfront. Only trouble is, a couple years ago, I came off my motorbike, and the MoD claimed I tried to top myself. Now they're withholding my pension. I didn't try anything – a car came round the corner – but they're keeping it anyway.' He looks up. 'My girlfriend doesn't know.'

'About the pension.'

'No.' He turns the bleed key. 'About Iraq.'

In the morning, I'm woken by the buzzing of my phone beside the bed. It's ten past seven on the clock. 'Hello,' I say. I hear the sound of a child splashing in the bath. 'Hello?' Then the call is ended.

I check my log. Toby's number.

An accidental call. I go back to sleep.

But when I open my bedroom door, a hot breeze laps at my legs and a fine layer of yellow sand eddies across the floor.

At half past eight, Toby appears carrying six-foot lengths of copper piping over his shoulder and a long hose looped over one arm. He deposits it all, heads out to the company van and returns, manoeuvring a wet-dry vacuum.

I boil the kettle. I don't mention the call. I don't mention the desert sand.

Today, it's another speech. His boss is a sadist. 'I'll move the radiator as per. That means I'll have to drain the radiators first, on both levels. Don't worry. I'll run the extractor hose outside. I'll also need to remove the rad nearest the front door – because it doesn't have a drain-off valve. I'll cut and relocate the pipework, reposition the radiator you want moved and make tight the compressed joint-work. The soldering will stink – sorry about that – but it will clear quickly if you open a few windows. I'll plumb the rad back up, fill the new system and add inhibitor. Then I'll bleed off the air, and fix a drain-off valve to make jobs easier in the future.' He consults a mental checklist. 'I'll lay a water blanket and will hoover any spillages. I'll leave it like I found it. Three to four hours' work. We don't paint the new pipework but I recommend the use of a primer.' Spit dribbles down his chin, and he turns to wipe it with his sleeve.

'Thank you,' I say.

His gums are red and vulnerable when he smiles. I can see the uncertainty in his eyes, now that he's clear of the speech. He's wondering if he said too much yesterday. I'm wondering too.

Upstairs in my kitchen, he leans against the banister, careful to avoid the laundry drying in the morning light. 'You'll be suntanning up here by August.'

Through my chapel window, we study the ridge of the Downs. The hills, the grass, the salt-bitten edges seem lit from within.

'You're going to need binoculars,' he adds.

The sea today is lagoon-green near the shore, turquoise where the shelf of England drops off and – deeper still, farther out – the fierce blue of the open Channel.

He is about to make a start on the drainage when it appears: the Portsmouth-to-Caen ferry, edging into view like a phantom ship. In outline, it looks too big, too bloated to be so close to shore.

'Shouldn't that be in the Solent?' he asks.

I nod. 'It passed the West Pier a few hours ago, adrift apparently. They were saying on the news. Just a skeleton crew. No passengers. I suppose it must still be going, carried on the tide.'

He squints into the day. 'Sounds like someone's big-whoops to me.'

'French ferry strike today. So the berth in Portsmouth is overfull, and they put this one to sea. No engines – to save fuel. They're calling it a "calculated drift".'

His smile is half grimace. 'Next time someone asks me what I'm up to, I'm going to borrow that. *Calculated drift*. "I'm in a calculated drift."'

We watch the lonely monolith of steel.

'Perhaps your girlfriend *should* know,' I say.

Two hours later, as the ferry drifts beyond my chapel arch, I call down the stairs. 'Almost gone.'

'God bless her,' he calls over his soldering torch, 'and all who forgot to sail in her!'

The stink of burnt metal rises. I heave windows open. 'Toby, you couldn't give me a hand, could you?' I forgot. Fresh laundry is everywhere. Sheets are drying over chairs, railings, my sofa, the kitchen table.

'I did warn you,' he calls.

'You did. So much for Lemon Fresh.' I reach for a sheet from the banister, pulling it up and across.

He goes to the stairs below, gets hold of the far edge and travels up, sparing it the dust of each step. 'My girl-friend can't keep house to save her life, but she's good with the kids and that, and she says they'll fuss in a few years if we're not married – sticklers for rules, kids are – so I did it. I booked the Registry Office.'

'Congratulations,' I say, beaming for him. 'That's lovely news.' I think of his broken mouth filled with vows.

'Second time round for me. When you're a marine, they say: marry desperate. Because anyone truly sane would have to be desperate to marry a Royal Marine. Anna, my ex, was out of my league. My own father said as much, but I ignored him. I was doolally for her.'

We shake out the sheet and pull it taut between us. Then we begin a quadrille of meetings and separations, slow at first, halting, until we find our momentum – reaching and folding, reaching and folding. When the sheet is reduced to a compact square of linen, we find ourselves stopped, hand to hand. 'They don't look it,' he says, 'but my hands are clean. The nails are only black where they didn't heal right after they were pulled.'

I blink. 'So you've set a date. That's wonderful.'

'She wants me to get dental implants first. She says, you only have one set of wedding photographs. I've told her about the last time, but she forgets, you know, on purpose like.'

I lay the folded sheet on the table, and he reaches for the next. Meet and fold. Meet and fold. 'I keep trying to explain there won't be any date if I have to pay for implants. And when I see my mouth, I'm fine with it. It reminds me – I got off easy.'

He turns his face to the vaulted ceiling and beams high over our heads. 'Original, those.' He points to the iron truss that runs the length of the kitchen and living room. 'And that. A single blacksmith made that. Not a foundry. A single man. Look at those iron knuckles. You could swing from that truss, and it wouldn't budge.'

'Sometimes,' I say, 'I stand here and imagine all those prayers downstairs in the old nave, a century's worth offered up.'

'It's peaceful here.' He nods. 'Solid.' Downstairs, among his tools, his phone buzzes but he ignores it. 'She was only ten in 2003. She knows I was a marine but she doesn't want details. The past is passed. Fair enough, I said. She said she thought she remembered it being on the news. The Invasion.'

We begin our quadrille again. The sheets in our hands hold the warmth of April. On my kitchen table, the tulips are risen. At the top of the chapel windows, the circular windows cast mandalas of light. A breeze moves through the skylight windows. Prayers roost in my roof space. Together we are Methodists.

Then Toby passes me the last sheet, grabs a blue corner and glances over the banister to check the drain-off hose downstairs. 'Your teeth,' he says, 'they're beautiful.'

★

That evening, the call comes around nine.

'Hello?' I say. I press my ear to a burble of voices and tinny, distant music. I wait, staring at my bedroom ceiling. 'Toby?'

The phone must be in his pocket. He's sitting on it. Down the pub.

I end the call.

In the night, beneath my chapel window, yellow sand drifts against the whitewashed walls. It piles high under the staircase.

At first light, I find the broom.

The new day brings taps and showerheads. Toby's been to the wholesalers'. I show him to the en suite where he checks the old taps a final time. 'Limescale, *end of*,' he says.

No speech today. He's broken free.

'In Stoke, where I grew up,' he tells me, 'the water is beautiful and soft.'

'Miss it?' I ask.

'Couldn't wait to get away, to join up.'

'And now?'

'I was married for years up there, and like I said, I've one teenage boy. I'm only down here because my girl-friend is a local girl. We met online. But being away seems to get harder, not easier, as you get older. Funny that.'

I nod. I see him as a boy, scrambling down the steep, stern valleys of the River Trent with his rod and box of bait, when he dreamed of seeing farther than the next valley.

'You? Family?' he asks.

'Not here.'

'Husband?' he asks.

'Divorced.'

'Significant Other?'

'Dead,' I say, '2003.'

'That bloody year again.' He unscrews the limescaled taps. 'Other Persons of Interest?'

I pass him a towel. 'That would be telling.'

He nods and turns to study the blocked showerhead. 'I thought you must be lonely. Betwixt and between. Now, me, I'd *pay* to be lonely. When I get home each night, like I said, it's a madhouse. And at weekends, my boys don't want to go out to fish with their old dad, not even when I say we'll put the boat on the water. I try to tidy up and join in with telly nights and that, but mostly I look around my house, and I think where am I? *Where the hell am I?* I go sit in Madison's room with a cup of tea or a brew. Sanity. You have to take it where you find it. Like yesterday. A customer in Lewes – you know Lewes? – he forgot to leave the keys.' He looks back to me and smiles shyly. 'Guess what I got up to?'

'Burned a cross?'

He looks at the floor and laughs. 'You're peculiar. I like that. I went to Anne of Cleves's House. No one else there. Had the run of the place. I like History. You like History?'

I smile. 'I like History.'

'Teacher? Lecturer?'

'Lecturer.'

'Thought so. No telly. All the books. Your moving men must have been glad to see the back of you.' He whistles. 'Lecturer. That's brave. If I had the choice between having to speak in public or having my fingers broken all over again, I know which I'd choose. Why do you think my teeth are like this? I asked someone once to smash them in, just to get me out of a job interview.'

My eyes widen. 'You didn't.'

He laughs again. 'Your face is a picture.' He looks away. 'A picture.'

In the en suite, we negotiate the narrow space. I look down, he looks up, we lift our ribcages and shuffle. I demonstrate the problem with the showerhead, the paltry spray. 'Low water pressure?'

We trade places and he clambers into the shower space. As he reaches up to the fitting, he appears, briefly, naked in my mind's eye, ready to soap an armpit. He's thirty-six. I did the maths. Younger than I realised, and older in himself than anyone should be. For a moment, he is a still photograph. A freeze-frame. No longer my plumber. I see the solemn gravity of his body, the dark energy of his pupils, the tenderness of his eyelashes and the truth in the unsteady line of his throat.

Toby strains higher to get a grip on the shower-head, but just as his spanner clamps on, his phone goes off. He passes me the spanner, hits 'Decline Call' and mimes, for my entertainment, the cutting of his own throat. 'My girlfriend. Who else?' When it rings again, a minute later, he climbs out of the shower, takes a seat on the loo and buries his eyes in his hand. 'No, love. Not yet. I'll be here a few more hours.'

I tidy the towels on the rack.

'Yes, it *is* a big job.'

I begin to slide past him, out of the room, but he shakes his head at me.

'Of course I haven't forgotten.' He murmurs into his phone. 'Yes, I *have* told her.'

Then he slides the mobile into his pocket and looks past my shoulder. 'Forgot to say. Doctor's appointment tomorrow. Not sure when they'll see me. Apparently, I just have to go along and hope.'

'Nothing serious?' It's what you say.

He massages a spot near his sternum. 'I've been hoping for months it would just go away. Right here. A lump. As big as fuck — sorry.' He looks up. He's spooked himself. 'Had a good look in the mirror the other week. I call it Saddam. It looks like him in profile.' From his perch on the toilet, he studies the showerhead again. 'I reckon somewhere in Basra there's a bloke with a tumour called Tony.' He extends his palm; I return the spanner. 'I just hope to Christ it's not breast cancer. My old navy mates would never let me live that one down.'

In the night, later than last time, my mobile rings. I hear a TV, a door closing, the scraping of a chair.

'Hello?' I try.

'Are you the one at the church?' a girl says.

'Who is this?' I say.

I know who it is.

'Is he with you? Is he there now?'

Outside my window, there's no moon. You wouldn't know there was a sea.

Bearings. Such delicate things.

I end the call.

In the morning, I rub the sand from my eyes. It crunches in my molars. Under my new showerhead, I rinse it from my hair and rub it from my scalp.

★

When Toby returns three days later, for the final job, the installation of a thermostat, he lowers his gear and a cardboard box to the floor, climbs my staircase and seats himself on the uppermost stair.

I follow him up and cock my head. 'So?'

'So?' he says, his face blank.

It's none of my business. 'What did the doctor say about Saddam?'

He bites the plastic packaging off the box. 'Moobs, yes, deffo. Breast cancer, no. No lung cancer either, as it happens.'

And the lump? I want to ask. *What about the lump?*

He opens the box, lifts out my new thermostat, and fishes for the installation instructions. He rummages in his toolbox, lifts out a glasses case and waves his specs. 'You'd never know I used to be a sniper.'

Watch.

A sniper is an expert marksman at a thousand yards. His vision is perfect or near perfect. When he isn't shooting, he is able to run three miles in eighteen minutes. He can perform a hundred sit-ups and twenty pull-ups in two minutes. He can execute the low crawl, medium crawl, high crawl and hand-and-knees crawl while carrying a hundred-pound pack, an L115A3 rifle and a 9mm pistol.

He can navigate by day and night. He can draw an accurate field sketch. He understands the vanishing point. He knows the imagination can distort. There can be no history of mental illness.

A sniper must move undetected. He must not smoke, move suddenly, use soap, wear insect repellent or arouse birds or wildlife. He relies on his spotter. The spotter will calculate wind velocity, the position of the sun, the grid coordinates and the range of all weapons prior to each shot.

On that searing March day in 2003, four men landed in the Drop Zone of Umm Qasr. 'Two teams,' Toby explains, 'in all that light. Two men too many.'

In desert areas, camouflage must be tan and brown.

A sniper uncovers his riflescope only when aiming at a target.

A sniper must not shine.

That day, Toby shone. While the four men lay prone on a rooftop across from the corner shop from which the target was about to emerge, Toby's St Jude medal slipped outside his T-shirt, outside his combats, and glinted in the midday light.

Later, in the concrete courtyard, the butt of an AK47 would break his skull and knock out his teeth. It would crush his fingers, break an arm and smash his ribs. Each day, the four men were pushed into the four chairs.

His first tour, his first assignment.

One morning, a bird, a warbler of some kind, sang overhead. *Kaka-kee, kaka-kee, kaka-kee.* Toby didn't hear the footsteps. Two shots rang out. Only when he opened his eyes did he understand he wasn't dead.

A scan revealed the lump on Toby's sternum to be a protective scar of bone; a final, slow mending where the ribs had rejoined the sternum.

I take a seat on the stair below him and stare straight ahead. 'How did you get out of the courtyard?'

He stalls, choosing his words for me. 'The two of us fought our way out.'

I understand what cannot be said to a stranger, in a stranger's new home. They killed their way out.

I don't turn around. 'Your girlfriend calls me,' I say, 'on your phone.'

'Ah,' he says. 'She say anything?'

'Not really.'

'Right,' he says.

'I suspect she knows you're keeping something from her.'

Behind me, he's nodding. Without turning, I know he's nodding. And staring at his hands.

'Another woman?' I try.

'Almost,' he says. I can hear the smile in his voice. 'Fatboy Slim.' He shifts on the stair. 'At night when it warms up like it has, I sneak out, pull on my waders and fish from his surf. No bathers to bother you, no one to see, and the bass bite best at night in spring and summer. I'm pretty good now at casting, hooking and landing them in the dark. Nice bloke actually. Don't expect he'd mind. I don't bother anyone. Before I leave, I hide my fish on the public side and return first thing to collect them, before work.'

'It seems you've been spotted. At home, I mean.'

'Point taken. Yep. After the kids are in bed, I slip out our back door. With her friends being over, I didn't think—' Behind me, I hear him rub his whiskered face. 'I leave my phone. I mute it and hide it under Madison's mattress. Can't risk it lighting up in the surf in the dark.'

'I'm fairly sure it wasn't Madison on the line.'

'No. Sorry. I'll sort it.'

'Maybe she knows you're keeping something more from her. More than the outings in the dark.'

'I am. As you know.' He hesitates. 'And it can keep. Now it can, I mean. That's what I mean. Now it can.'

'Right,' I say. 'That's good,' I say.

I feel his hand, light, fleeting, on my shoulder. 'You're a fine Methodist woman.'

I turn back and peer up. His grin is broad.

'That's a comfort.' I bite back a smile. 'But I forgot to say. Our tulips are dead. I mean, totally dead this time.'

He sighs. 'Total death. It comes to us all in the end. Including the two *beautiful* bass I landed last night.' His smile breaks out again. 'They're on ice in the back of the van. Not gutted yet, but I could give you one if you like.'

'You're all right,' I say. 'Next time maybe.'

I look away again.

And together, beneath my chapel window, we sit in pools of morning shadow and light while, somewhere beyond its bright panes, the Portsmouth-to-Caen ferry is slowly returned to port.

all the beloved ghosts

For Angelica Garnett 1918–2012

Angelica passes through the bow-ceilinged kitchen – or 'the green room' as the assistant at her side refers to it. Her eyebrow, or what remains of it after ninety years, arches at the phrase. The kitchen is the *kitchen*. More to the point, it has been whitewashed for as long as she can remember. If she is demented – and the whispering of her ageing children would have her believe as much – at least she can testify to the colour of her family's former kitchen. If she is gaga, at least she has the manners to walk *around*, rather than *through*, the dead.

Grace, specifically.

At the great, hulking square of a table, Grace, the housekeeper of her childhood years, is slender and pink-faced again. She pours tea from the ancient yellow pot with the cracked glaze, and steamy bergamot rises on the air. *Wherever did that pot get to?* Angelica wonders. An assortment of cups and saucers wait on two trays. A silver tea strainer lies by the milk jug – which means there will be no giddy reading of the tea leaves this afternoon by the children; no stolen glimpses of the future, and really, Angelica decides, that is just as well. Doesn't the future rush at you headlong? Doesn't it get hold of your heart and—

THUMP-THUMP-thump. There it is again. Upstairs, above the bulging ceiling, footsteps beat out their metre, a sound she knows in the depths of herself, like something rolling at the bottom of an old trunk. The feet are too quick in their step for middle age, too heavy for a child's.

Julian. She is sure of it. The girl assistant at her side wouldn't understand, of course she wouldn't, but never mind the girl. *Oh, Julian, we were never ourselves again without you.*

'Mrs Garnett, may I get you anything before we make our way to the marquee?'

My brother. My brother who died in a stalemate of a battle in a place whose name I can't remember.

The girl's high-browed oval face is tipped to one side. It is a pretty face, certainly, but unremarkable, Angelica decides. It boasts all the blandness of good breeding. (Her daughters tell her she mustn't use the phrase 'good breeding'. They assure her it is offensive these days, but offensive to whom? Horses?)

If the girl and her face disappoint, Angelica can admit, privately, that her vowels are pleasingly rounded and resonant. She could not fail to appreciate their music. It conjures images of broderie anglaise, of almond party favours and of clean white napkins dropped into the lap. But for all that, Angelica is not interested in the girl. And – *oh, oh* – Julian's footsteps overhead have – she listens again – gone.

But the quiet, the composure of Grace's routine in the kitchen has the restoring effect of a Vermeer. Grace arranges wedges of lemon on a plate and adds a pair of tongs. She lays oatcakes for Duncan and stacks of freshly buttered toast for the children. She selects ripe plums from the willow basket on the floor and piles them high in a bowl for Vanessa's pleasure. The plums are the colour of a Sussex sky before a downpour, and in this moment as Angelica gazes, she falls *into* their colour, into a dark pool of plumminess.

When she surfaces, she finds that Grace's ghost is also standing utterly still, her eyes closed, her face as contented as a Sufi at prayer. But Grace is not similarly moved by the plums; she is warming her backside in front of the coal range. It is a private moment of course, and she, Angelica, is trespassing.

The girl assistant and her even-featured face are waiting. What can Angelica do but bow her head, take her cane and follow the girl out the side door? *Not* that this guarantees they will be on time. Audience or no audience, she will not be hurried.

So they get only as far as the old cattle pond at the front of the house when she stops again, seduced by its light. The breeze ruffles the surface. She wanders to the edge and locates her image in the upside-down world, discovering the girl who used to stand in that spot. She blinks at herself through the wrinkled glass, across decades and dimensions. Behind the barn, the milking machine grinds preternaturally to life, and a cow bellows. Swallows snip the afternoon sky.

Another day gone.

She turns at last and follows the girl whose name she can't recall – Sophie or Zoë or Chloë. Her hand reaches out, a reflex action, to push on the door that leads into the walled garden, but the old, familiar door is gone. She hears only the phantom creak of its hinges. On either side of the path, hollyhocks – huge and fantastic-al – nod to her on the breeze.

The girl leads the way, turning at intervals. It is her job to get her to the marquee on time, and it is, no doubt, a challenge. Earlier Angelica insisted that she did not want a retinue, nor even as much as an elbow to clutch.

She wanted only to be alone with the house, her old family home, to be where visitors, where others, were not. She wanted to feel again the warmth of its floorboards beneath her feet; to see the bright chintz curtains blowing in the breeze. Perhaps she'd unearth her earliest sketches, drawn with lumps of chalk her brothers had gathered for her on the Downs all those years ago. She'd dawdle over memories of poached eggs made from daisies for her rag doll; of the River Cuck icy between her toes; of the old bay tree in whose branches she once balanced, small but queenly.

'Mind this bit here, Mrs Garnett,' Chloë calls over her shoulder. She taps the offending flagstone with her foot.

Angelica nods curtly to demonstrate good sense. But the day, the house and its ghosts do not make it easy. Far from it. On the garden lawn by the ornamental pond, she must try not to look too closely at the ensemble of children in costume, at the girl and her brothers who are posed in the tragic attitude of a *tableau vivant*. Their arms implore. Their eyes are woebegone. Their mouths tremble with giggles.

She remembers the Grecian-style dress. Her mother ran it up for her on the Singer. It was once a sheet on the floor of the attic studio; if the girl were to turn, Angelica knows she would see telltale splashes of Prussian blue paint on the back. And if she were to speak to her ten-year-old self, what should happen then?

The child would no doubt be frightened by so old a person; by the need to speak closely to a fuzzy, overgrown ear. How could Angelica tell her to *Take it all in, remember, because life pares you down and . . .*

In that moment, a figure passes so near to her, she catches the whiff of turpentine from the pores of his jacket.

The shadow over her heart disappears.

Duncan.

He is carrying a bundle of roses he has cut himself. He takes a penknife from his pocket, flays a stem of its thorns and, without disturbing the girl's pose, slips a white bloom behind her ear.

'It smells of cold cream!' she says, laughing.

'Careful,' he teases. 'You're wrinkling your nose. Quentin, your director brother, will not be pleased.'

'Mrs Garnett?' Zoë again.

'It's nothing,' she says. 'Something in my eye. An eyelash.'

Zoë assures her that they are nearly at the marquee, as if she is unable to mark their progress for herself. Doddering. Doolally. Angelica prefers the term 'demented'. It has a certain drama. It suggests a capacity for danger.

'Are you fine to go on?'

'Yes, yes,' she mutters, with a fluttering of her hand. But, in spite of the girl's fervent hope that she will come along, and in spite of her own blasé assurances, as they step into what was once the orchard, she stumbles.

Her neck jolts back, her stomach lurches, and only at the last moment does her cane anchor her. Her ankle rights itself after all. She does not hit the ground. The wind is not knocked from her. Her free hand flies to the beads at her neck, as if they are a rope thrown to her in the tide.

Relax, she commands herself, *relax*. She has not embarrassed herself with a fall. Her hip will not crack today.

She is aware that – Chloë? – has paused on the path; that the girl is trying very hard not to make a fuss. Her wide, milky brow is wrinkling with concern for an elderly woman, for a weathered castaway adrift in a new century. How can Angelica possibly explain?

Vanessa. *There.* At her easel.

In the orchard of all places.

She hadn't expected her mother, at this late stage of things, to subscribe to any notion of an afterlife. It's a rather cruel joke. Before her death, Vanessa flatly refused to avail herself of a vicar, a funeral service and even of mourners. Didn't she show contempt for everything but a hole in the ground? Why leave your loved ones in so stark a place? Why be so remote? Why not cooperate in death if not in life?

Angelica feels the old molten force blast within her, and her eyes fill with hot tears.

It is trite to blame one's mother, as is her wont, especially when one's mother is long dead. What a spoiled child she sometimes seems, even to herself. And of course she *was* spoiled, everyone says she was, why even *books* say she was, though surely so much freedom for a child is a form of neglect, is it not?

It occurs to Angelica that the mother before her now is a woman of just forty-odd years again, almost half a century younger than she herself. Vanessa simply has no right to be alive and painting here in the orchard. Nor has she the right, after so many years gone, to stand before her daughter, still unaware, still so absorbed, and so vivid it is as if *she*, Angelica, is the ghost, the lesser presence, the trick of the light.

'Mrs Garnett, do you need a moment?'

Vanessa is of course indifferent to both Sophie and Angelica. She always had the gift of utter concentration. She is not distracted by ghosts from the future. Angelica watches her mother daub the oils on her canvas with a palette knife. When Vanessa bends to adjust the easel, her palms flash out, a blur of green, ochre and black. Her subject is a fallen apple. She is drawn to the bravura of its rot.

'Almost time, Mrs Garnett,' chimes Sophie.

She won't offer Sophie Augustine's thoughts on time. She won't explain that time comes out of the future, which does not yet exist, into the present, which has no duration, and into the past, which has ceased to be.

Her mother paints on. She is wearing her long brown velvet coat. The buttons fell off years ago. She has rolled up the sleeves. A patch of saffron yellow marks one of the coat's elbows. She does not turn to acknowledge her daughter, and it is, Angelica tells herself, for the best.

She accepts Zoë's elbow.

'I believe they're ready for you, Mrs Garnett.'

She shakes out her shoulders. She tells Zoë that she is accustomed to making a spectacle of herself; that she has always been good at play-acting. Once upon a time, when she was a girl, she posed as a Russian princess for one of her Aunt Virginia's stories. This particular story was to have pictures. Photographs. Her aunt explained that she should imagine the princess character as if she is like the waves of the sea when you look down upon them from up high, or as a hill, all green with spring-time, but glimpsed through clouds.

Angelica stops and turns to Zoë. 'Do *you* have any idea what that means?'

Zoë smiles and shakes her head.

'I tried hard not to frown, but my aunt was not help-ing at all. It was only when Leonard winked at me from above his camera – I *adored* Leonard – that, suddenly, I knew how to do it. I slipped the fur cloak over my shoulders and put the hat upon my head. I assumed the sombre expression of a girl who is both burdened and made beautiful by Destiny.'

She checks Zoë's face, expecting her to smile, expect-ing her to find it unimaginable that the old woman on her arm might once have been capable of beauty. But Zoë betrays no trace of incredulity.

Perhaps she has seen the pictures. Postcards in the gift shop. Images from photo albums in the online archive. All their dear faces – zoom, zoom, magnify – made startlingly clear and strange.

She must remember to finish her stories. 'It was for the lovely, silly novel,' she says.

As Zoë ushers her into the marquee, the hum of the crowd whooshes in her ear. She leans towards the girl, and her smile is wry: 'But I'd make only the flimsiest of characters now.'

At the steps to the stage, she has to bend so low that her torso is almost parallel to the floor. She grips the brass top of her cane with one hand and a courteous male forearm with the other. After her stumble in the orchard, she fears her legs are mutinous.

When she manages the ascent, she lets herself drop into a high-backed chair at centre stage. She straightens herself as much as nature will allow.

Is that her aunt in the front row?

Of course it isn't. It is her niece. She knows that. But the resemblance does not help.

Someone, the owner of the courteous male fore-arm, is introducing her from the lectern. The show has started, it would seem, and she is the show. She hears that she was born in the house on Christmas Day 1918; that she is an accomplished artist in her own right. She wonders where Sophie has got to.

'Many of you will know that Angelica Garnett, in addition to being a talented painter, is also a gifted museum.' Above the microphone, her host blushes deeply. 'A gifted *musician,* I should say.'

She smiles devilishly, and the audience laugh. Poor chap, she thinks, he got it right the first time. She is only too aware that she is an old lady with red-rimmed eyes. Her long painter's hands are a mountain range of veins. Her hair is a silver bob. In spite of the warmth of the day, she wears an oversized pullover, a dark woollen skirt, brown loafers and bright blue socks.

She is enjoying herself now. She is not *un*interesting. How many people, after all, can say they married their father's lover?

Only two glasses of water and a low table separate her from her interviewer. He has a high dome of a head, and his reading glasses dangle casually, confidently, from one hand. She understands he is a biographer. Much of the time, she doesn't know the answers these people want.

They will never know, for example, about the elegy unfolding within her for the moorhens of her

childhood and their beautiful red bills; for the gleaming beetles and the hairy green gooseberries; for the
Roorkhee chairs on the terrace where the adults would
sit at twilight; for the day that Roger's hat was lost, and
everyone, even Duncan's new model, was enlisted by
Vanessa to search – the model with only a small towel
around his waist.

These moments cannot be panned like gold from
the past, or if they can, they cannot be held.

Q: Can you hear me, Angelica?

A: Speak a little louder, if you would.

Q: We're here at Charleston, your childhood home and
the home of your parents, the painters Vanessa Bell and
Duncan Grant. Would you say a little about what it was
that attracted Vanessa to Duncan as a painter?

A: His wit. His gaiety, I suppose. (Pause.) They painted
together, often the same subject, though something
quite different would come out with each.

Q: Did they offer each other criticism?

A: I suppose so, but their criticism was very practical.

Q: Practical in what sort of way?

A: 'You should use that blue.'

Q: I see.

A: 'That line should go there.' (The audience laugh. She
has deflated his well-informed question.)

Q: Was Vanessa dependent on Duncan as a painter?

A: One hears she was.

Q: Perhaps he 'freed up' her style?

A: I'm afraid you'd have to ask her (*there at her easel, in the orchard even as we speak*).

Q: Virginia and Leonard were of course frequent visitors. What was Virginia's relationship with Duncan?

A: Rather friendly, I think. Not very, very close. Well, because he was a painter and she was a writer.

Q: And Leonard and Duncan?

A: I think Leonard was slightly irritated by Duncan – not that it showed. Everyone would have pretended whatever the case.

Q: It was in the Garden Room that Vanessa, your mother, told you that Duncan Grant, not Clive Bell, was actually your biological father. Is that right?

A: Is that what they call it now? Yes, I was seventeen, I believe. Seventeen or eighteen. I suppose you could tell me. I'm afraid Vanessa made the wrong decision when I was born and then, I daresay, couldn't get out of it . . .

Q: In spite of the general agreement *not* to tell you the truth for many years, was Duncan a 'father figure' as you grew up?

A: No. He was generous and kind, certainly, but he had no authority. It wasn't in his nature. Leonard was a father figure of sorts. Not Duncan.

Q: Do you find it odd that we seem to be acquainted with your relatives on a first-name basis?

A: Yes, I suppose I do.

The minutes pass. The words come out of her, like a script she knows rather too well. Rain begins to tap on the canvas overhead and somewhere a lapwing cries.

Q: Did you have animals here as a child?

A: Yes, I had a cocker spaniel. And, before you ask, I had a reasonably good relationship with it! (More audience laughter.) It was given me by Vita Sackville-West, who bred them. Blotto or Botto . . .

Her attention is directed to the audience. She straightens herself in her chair. A tall, masculine sort of woman stands and adjusts the scarf on her shoulder before reaching for the mic.

Q: May I ask, did you see the film *The Hours*, and if so what did you think of Nicole Kidman's portrayal of Virginia?

A: A film, you say? I'm afraid I don't get to the pictures much. (She is feeling impish now.) Was I in it?

A long-faced man in specs and a waistcoat takes the mic.

Q: It seems to me that Maynard Keynes was one of the truly great minds of the last century. As a child, what were your impressions of him?

A: Maynard was charming. He wasn't particularly interested in me but I remember that when I was small, he used to come into the bath and shower me in bath salts!

The long-faced man chews his lip and takes his seat. The mic travels to a woman in a red cardigan.

Q: Angelica, I wonder, do you ever *dream* of Charleston?

The woman has a beautiful voice, as soothing as a Beethoven sonata.

A: Do I ever dream of Charleston?

Q: Yes . . .

And for no reason at all, she feels her thoughts eddy; her hands tighten on the arms of her chair, as if she might slip into herself and not surface again.

She has to reach for her glass of water and clear her throat. Her questioner doesn't know whether to remain standing or to take her seat, and the audience wait, anxious on an elderly woman's behalf. In the front row, her niece's eyes (and simultaneously her aunt's) widen.

Do you ever dream of Charleston?

She dabs her eyes with the cuff of her pullover, and as she does so, she notices Sophie. Yes, it *is* Sophie. That's where she's got to. She is standing at the back of the tent, directly within her line of sight, and she is nodding to her, her face as benign as a Madonna's. *Dear* Sophie and her *dear* Madonna face.

Angelica lifts her chin and speaks to Sophie.

'I do. I do dream of Charleston. For many years, it was the same dream. The house was on fire and everyone was rushing around like ants. There was such confusion, such . . . chaos. But lately it's different. We're all gone. I can see *deep* rooms. The bricks are freshly whitewashed. The windows are open. The floor-boards are bare and striped with sunlight. Each room is empty – of furniture, books, paintings – and dust is streaming, everywhere there's dust, but – how can I explain it? – it's golden. Endless. And we're *gone*: me, you, all the beloved ghosts, all of us.'

Acknowledgements

I would like to thank the wonderful team at Bloomsbury UK and USA, and especially Nigel Newton, Alexandra Pringle, Angelique Tran Van Sang and Anton Mueller. I'm very grateful, too, to Nicole Winstanley at Hamish Hamilton Canada. I'm fortunate to have world-class talent at work in support of this book.

I'd also like to thank my ever impressive agent, David Godwin, and everyone at DGA, including Heather Godwin, Kirsty McLachlin, Philippa Sitters and Lisette Verhagen.

My warmest thanks are also due to writer friends Karen Stevens and Hugh Dunkerley. Their sharp eyes have helped these stories come to life. Equally, I'd like to thank my friend, Professor Denis Noble, who was incredibly generous in our collaboration as I wrote 'The Heart of Denis Noble'.

I am grateful, too, to the late Angelica Garnett. I was moved to write the story 'all the beloved ghosts' after hearing her speak, twice, at the special place that is the Charleston Farmhouse in East Sussex. Her art was one inspiration for the story, as was her memoir, *Deceived with Kindness*. I feel privileged that she took the time to read the story in 2010 and to allow publication.

Regarding my 'Chekhov trio', I am, like most story writers, indebted to the inspiration of Chekhov, his life and his fiction. I'd also like to acknowledge and thank Chekhov biographers Donald Rayfield and Rosamund Bartlett, and editor/translator of the Chekhov–Knipper letters, Jean Benedetti.

In the story 'In Praise of Radical Fish', the extract cited by Hamid is taken from the *Rubaiyat of Omar Khayyam* (translated by Edward Fitzgerald).

I'd like to thank the following editors, producers and publishers for their generous support and for first publication/broadcast of versions of many of the stories collected here: editor Kate Pullinger and Bloomsbury UK for 'The Thaw' in *Waving at the Gardener* (Bloomsbury); producer Jeremy Osborne of Sweet Talk Productions for 'Solo, A Cappella', first broadcast in shorter form on BBC Radio 4; publisher Ra Page of Comma Press who commissioned 'The Heart of Denis Noble' for *Litmus: Short Stories from Modern Science*; editor A. J. Ashworth who commissioned 'Sylvia Wears Pink in the Underworld' for *Matter Magazine*; Editor-of-Readings at the BBC Di Speirs and producer Elizabeth Allard who commissioned 'There are precious things' for BBC Radio 3; editor Peter Wild who commissioned 'Oscillate Wildly' for *Paint a Vulgar Picture: Fiction Inspired by the Smiths* (Serpent's Tail); editor Barbara Marshall who published a very early version of 'Dreaming Diana: Twelve Frames' in *Reading Prose* (Hodder & Stoughton); Sweet Talk Productions and Jeremy Osborne for commissioning 'In Praise of Radical Fish' for BBC Radio 4; Tom Vowler and Anthony Caleshu, editors of the journal *Short Fiction*, who first published a version of 'all the beloved ghosts'; and finally, once again, producer Jeremy Osborne of Sweet Talk and Commissioning Editor Caroline Raphael at BBC Radio 4 for the commission of my 'Imagining Chekhov' trio of stories.

Funding from both the Eccles Centre for American Studies at the British Library and the Society of Authors' Authors' Foundation helped to provide the vital time for me to complete this book. I am enormously grateful to both organisations.

Alison MacLeod
May 2016

A Note on the Author

Alison MacLeod was born in Canada and has lived in the UK since 1987. She is the author of three novels, *The Changeling*, *The Wave Theory of Angels* and *Unexploded*, which was longlisted for the Man Booker Prize for Fiction 2013, and a collection of stories, *Fifteen Modern Tales of Attraction*. Alison MacLeod is the joint winner of the 2016 Eccles British Library Writer's Award. She is Professor of Contemporary Fiction at the University of Chichester and lives in Brighton.

alison-macleod.com

A Note on the Type

The text of this book is set in Bembo, which was first used in 1495 by the Venetian printer Aldus Manutius for Cardinal Bembo's *De Aetna*. The original types were cut for Manutius by Francesco Griffo. Bembo was one of the types used by Claude Garamond (1480–1561) as a model for his Romain de l'Université, and so it was a forerunner of what became the standard European type for the following two centuries. Its modern form follows the original types and was designed for Monotype in 1929.